LEVIATHAN

LEVIATHAN

By
Dr. Tim Scott

SWORD of the LORD PUBLISHERS

P. O. Box 1099, Murfreesboro, TN 37133

Printed and Bound in the United States of America

Contents

Chapter 1
RUMBLINGS

Dr. Samuel Walker stepped out of his car and into the bitter January wind. He ran the thirty or so steps to the front door of his apartment building. As he opened the door, a wave of warmth hit him, causing him to gasp even harder for breath. But he didn't mind the blast of warm air. He pulled off his snow-covered coat and hat and carried them up to his second-floor apartment.

He unlocked his apartment door and stepped inside. "Sammy, is that you?" he heard his wife, Janet, call from the kitchen.

"Yeah, just me, the Abominable Snowman. What are you doing here?"

Janet walked into the living room holding a mixing bowl. "I live here from time to time, remember?" she said, her eyes twinkling. "Why? Disappointed?"

"No, of course not," replied Dr. Walker, chuckling. "I'm glad to see you. But aren't you supposed

1

to be assisting Dr. Blair with his freshman chemistry lab this afternoon? Or is that some kind of experiment you're stirring?"

Janet laughed. "Well, it is kind of an experiment. It's your dinner. As for the class, the snowstorm killed that. They've rescheduled for Friday."

Dr. Walker walked over to Janet and kissed her. "How come they never reschedule *my* classes? And what's for dinner?"

"A new casserole recipe, and don't ask. When you get a recipe from a botanist, you're in for a real adventure. Better just to eat it and decide. And you never get rescheduled because you teach senior classes. You know that."

Dr. Walker followed his wife back to the kitchen. "For once, I wish they would just cancel the rest of the semester," he said. "I can't stand it anymore. And with finals a week away, classes are just interference. If the students don't have it by now, I certainly can't help them this last week. And this weather! What I wouldn't give for a nice trip south of the equator right now!"

Janet put down the bowl with a thump. She turned to her husband. "You are NOT going to Africa. Period."

Dr. Walker jumped. "Africa? What do you mean?"

"You know, jungles and grasslands. Big animals. Africa."

2

"But I never said anything about going to Africa. I haven't been to Africa for ten years." Dr. Walker's expression changed from shock to curiosity. "What are you talking about?"

Janet smiled, wiped her hands on her apron, and said, "I'll be right back." She walked out of the kitchen toward the bedroom. When she returned, she was holding a small box. She held it out to her husband. "This came today. It's from Clyde Derrington. And you're NOT going to Africa."

Dr. Walker took the box and began ripping off the brown wrapping paper. "I wasn't even sure Clyde was still in Africa. The last time I heard from him, he was trying to start a mission station in the Interior. I wonder what this could be. Must have cost a fortune to mail it."

Janet pulled up a chair and sat down beside her excited husband. She was also curious about the package. Clyde Derrington had been Samuel's best friend in college. Samuel had been an education major, and Clyde, a missions major. Samuel had often said Clyde was the best Christian he knew. "That guy really cares about people," Samuel had told her. "He honestly, really cares about their eternal future. And he's going to do something about it. Just watch him. I expect him to do something great for God."

And it was true. Clyde had been a pastor on the

mission field for nearly ten years, and he had seen hundreds of natives come to trust Christ as Saviour. His newest endeavor was an attempt to establish a mission station nearly five hundred miles from the nearest city, in the heart of southern Africa. He wanted to reach people who had never even heard of Jesus Christ.

Dr. Walker was trembling with excitement and having difficulty with the well-wrapped package. Janet gently took it from him. She went to her utility drawer and took out a small pair of scissors. In just a few seconds, she had the package open. In it were a letter and a small plastic instant coffee jar sealed with strapping tape. It contained a whitish, almost yellow liquid.

"Yuck," said Janet. "What is this?"

"I don't know," replied Dr. Walker, looking closely at the thick fluid. "Maybe he explains in the letter." While he opened the envelope Janet busied herself trying to open the jar.

"Shall I read it aloud?" he asked.

"Yes."

> **Marjao Station, Uganda**
> **Dear Samuel,**
>
> **Greetings in the name of our Lord Jesus Christ.**
>
> **It has been a long time since we have written, and I have intended to do so often. Please forgive my tardiness in corresponding...**

Janet looked up from the jar. "Like he has nothing else to do."

"Really."

Dr. Walker continued reading:

> Strange happenings here have prompted my letter. I will explain as best I can, though I am really at a loss for an explanation.
>
> Several months ago we started receiving opposition from the natives concerning our attempts to build an infirmary. They had allowed us to build quarters for ourselves—that is, my wife and me, the Steven Johnsons, and our native servant, Jendel. They were actually quite excited when we built a chapel, and they have been faithful to attend services. They are very open to the Bible, and several have trusted Christ as their Saviour. And you should hear them sing!
>
> But when we started to build a small clinic, they suddenly balked. Some of the older ones said we had angered the jungle spirits by our coming. They tried to keep the young parents from bringing their children for much-needed medical treatment. And they threatened to burn the infirmary if we continued to build it.
>
> When I asked them to explain what was happening and why they thought the "jungle spirits" were unhappy, they looked terrified. They were not just giving us trouble; they were actually frightened. Some of the women cried when I pressed them for an explanation. They would not answer me directly. They would only tell me that they were afraid they were going to be killed.
>
> Finally, Jendel was able to convince one old man to give him some information. They trust Jendel because they consider him one of

them. At least, he is better accepted than we are. This old man told Jendel that a creature called Burong had attacked a village far to the west of a lake he called Nyvasu. I had never heard of the lake, and apparently the map makers haven't either! It is a small lake in the jungle, somewhere in the Great Rift Valley. I have tried to gain more information, but all I can learn is that it is about twenty miles from here.

Jendel could not get any information about the Burong. I do not know if the name Burong is supposed to be a kind of animal or if it is the name of a specific creature. But I know the name carries a lot of significance with the natives. If you just say the word, they will cower in fear and beg you not to talk about it. Very strange.

Last night I heard loud voices outside the infirmary. Then I heard something hitting the window. When I went outside, several natives whom I did not recognize ran away into the jungle. They had strange green markings on their skin and were wearing yellow feathers in their hair.

When I looked at the window, it had been pelted with the stuff that's in the jar I sent you. I have no idea what it is. I hope it's not too rich by the time it arrives. I had no way to keep it refrigerated in transit, and I know it'll take at least three weeks to get to you. You may not even want to open it!

One more thing. When Jendel showed the stuff to the old man, the old fellow nearly fainted. Then he said, "Burong."

I hope you can shed some light on this for me. The whole affair is really setting our work back. Our congregation has shrunk to just our converts. We can't get the other natives to come. Apparently, the Burong trouble began

when we started on the infirmary, and we can't convince them we're not responsible.

Let me know something as soon as possible. Thanks.

In Christ,
Clyde Derrington

Janet pulled the last of the tape off the jar. She looked up at her husband. "Well?"

"I don't think we'd better open it tonight. I'll take it to the lab tomorrow and see if I can figure out what it is."

"Thanks, Sammy," said Janet. "That casserole is going to be hard enough to eat after that story without smelling up the kitchen with this stuff."

Dr. Walker looked at the casserole. "Let's order pizza."

"Yes, let's," said Janet, putting the jar down carefully on the table. "And by the way—"

"What?"

"You're NOT going to Africa."

Chapter 2
EMERGENCY

The next morning, Dr. Samuel Walker returned to his office at Michigan Christian University with new vigor, a renewed ambition—and a jar of slime.

He avoided everyone he could, not trying to be impolite but simply trying to hurry to his laboratory. He wanted to examine the sample sent to him by Clyde Derrington before it disintegrated any further. Without breaking stride he threw his coat across his office chair, dropped his hat on his desk and hurried down the hallway to the zoology lab.

When he entered the lab, he turned on the bright lights and settled himself on a stool in front of a dissecting table. Thinking about the possible odor that would be released when he opened the jar, he switched on the overhead vent and turned on the water in the sink. If the slime proved corrosive, he wanted to be able to rinse the sink quickly.

Dr. Walker put on an apron, a pair of rubber gloves and protective glasses. Then, slowly, he opened the jar. The odor that escaped was offensive but not overpowering. "Definitely organic," he muttered to himself. "Looks like an excretion, perhaps mucus of some kind. I'm sure it must have deteriorated somewhat."

Just then the lab door opened behind him. "Sam?" It was the voice of his elderly friend and colleague, Dr. Horace Atteberry.

"Hi, Doc," said Dr. Walker, without turning around. "Come here a minute. I want to show you something. Oh, better grab some gloves and a mask."

Dr. Atteberry donned his protective gear. "What are you doing here so early?" he asked as he shuffled over to the table. "And what is that awful smell? Oh, what is that stuff?"

"Very unprofessional, Doc," chuckled Dr. Walker. "It's not stuff—it's slime."

"Oh, yes, my mistake. I should have recognized that important distinction right away. But what is it?"

"I don't know. How's that for an answer?"

"Good for starters, I guess. What do you think it is?"

Dr. Walker explained the entire incident to Dr. Atteberry, who was also acquainted with Clyde Derrington and his mission work. "Now *I'm* hooked," said Dr. Atteberry when the narrative was finished. "May I?" and with that, he picked up the

jar. He ladled some of the foul-smelling slime onto a slide and placed a cover slide over it. He turned on a microscope and placed the slide in its holder.

"Well, it is definitely organic, and it's evidently some kind of mucus excretion. Looks to me like snail slime."

"That's what I thought," said Dr. Walker, "but have you ever seen so much snail slime in one place?"

"No," said Dr. Atteberry. His wrinkled forehead settled into even deeper lines, and he removed his spectacles as he thought. "And you say this is just a sample. There was more where this came from?"

"A lot more," said Dr. Walker. "So what does that tell us?"

"It might tell us something about the Burong. We might be dealing with a giant slug or snail of some kind."

"Big enough to scare a whole village?"

"Hmm, good point. But it's got to be some kind of animal that lays down mucus—that is, if the natives are correct in associating this slime with their unknown beast."

"They seemed pretty sure, Doc."

"Sounds like it," agreed the older professor. "Sam, let's send part of this sample up to the biochemistry department. We won't tell them what we think it is. Let's get a chemical analysis and see if it really is snail mucus."

"Good idea, Doc. In the meantime, let's try to keep this thing quiet. If everyone finds out about it, our story will prejudice the results of the chemical analysis. I don't want those guys up there to know what it is they have. Let's make them tell us what it is, based on its chemical composition alone."

The two professors placed a sample of the slime in a clean container and filled out a request form. They sent the request through the regular channels so no one would suspect that the sample was anything unusual. By noon, the sample had arrived at biochemistry.

Late that afternoon their analysis arrived in Dr. Walker's e-mail. He printed it out and looked at the summary.

> The material which was sent to us
> for analysis from the zoology
> department, requested by Drs. Atte-
> berry and Walker, namely, sample
> number ZB-41420, consists of a
> protein-based material unlike any
> encountered in our experience. We
> ran a cross-check of its structure
> against the databases of the Bio-
> Gen internet site and found no
> exact match. The partial matches
> include mammalian nasal secretions

```
and slug or snail "foot" excre-
tions. The material more closely
resembles the latter, but is not an
exact match. Please read detailed
analysis on following pages for more
information.
```

A second e-mail followed. This was personal mail for Dr. Walker from Dr. Irving Drummond, head of the biochemistry department. It read: "Sammy, where did you get this stuff? Irving."

Dr. Atteberry walked in just as Dr. Walker was removing the second note from his laser printer. Dr. Walker handed his colleague the report. "Thought so. But it's strange that even Bio-Gen couldn't place it. I thought they had a file on everything ever discovered."

"Maybe they did, until now," said Dr. Walker. "I think maybe we've run into something new. And, by the way, I stand corrected. Irving agrees with your terminology."

"What's that?" Dr. Atteberry took the second e-mail from Dr. Walker. He read the short note and laughed. "I feel vindicated. It was 'stuff.' Of course, it's also slime. Just a matter of semantics. Now what shall we call it?"

"I don't know," Dr. Walker said as he walked to his chair and sat down. "Do you think we're really dealing with a giant snail here? I feel like Dr.

Doolittle even talking about it."

Dr. Atteberry sat down opposite his friend. "There are too few mysteries left on the planet, Sam. This one intrigues me. Of course, I've always had an interest in unknown and mysterious animals. I suppose every zoologist does. In fact, for many years I dreamed of having enough money that I wouldn't have to work. I'd just follow every lead until I could find just one of the world's mystery creatures. Just one firsthand sighting of the Bigfoot or, you know, to photograph the Loch Ness Monster..." His voice drifted off into his dreams.

"Yeah, I know," agreed Dr. Walker. "I've never had the courage to come right out and get involved in cryptozoology, but I've dreamed about it. The closest I ever came to being involved in unknown animals was the final in your invertebrates class. I didn't know half of them!"

Dr. Atteberry laughed. "It was a great day for all us crackpot professors when somebody invented the term 'cryptozoology.' Now we can look for dinosaurs or sea monsters or hairy men all we want, and nobody laughs at us. We just claim to be trying to solve the last of the planet's mysteries. When we give ourselves a ten-dollar name, they stop calling us lunatics."

"Well, I'd like to find out what's going on at Lake Nyvasu. And it's not just my professional curiosity. It's not even unprofessional curiosity.

I've got a friend down there who needs help. And it will drive me crazy until I hear it's been resolved."

"Then why don't you go?"

"How? I don't have the money to finance an expedition like that. And I've got classes to teach. Besides," continued Dr. Walker, his face breaking into a grin, "Janet says, 'You're NOT going to Africa.'"

Dr. Atteberry grinned in response. "You can handle Janet."

"*My* Janet?"

Just then the phone rang. Dr. Walker picked it up. "Okay, thanks, Vicki," he said at length. "I'll come get it." With that, Dr. Walker jumped to his feet and hurried to his office door. There he paused just long enough to say, "I'll be right back." Then he hurried to the receptionist's desk and picked up a telegram.

When Dr. Walker returned to his office, Dr. Atteberry looked up. "Everything all right?"

"I don't know, Doc. This telegram is from Clyde. It must have been an emergency for him to send a telegram. Let me get it open, and I'll tell you."

He read the telegram aloud:

> **Sam, urgent for you to come. Left mission station due to reasons stated in previous letter. Work at standstill. Please come. I need you here—Clyde.**

"What do you think, Doc?" he asked, handing the telegram to his friend.

Dr. Atteberry did not answer for a moment. "I think you ought to talk to Janet again, Sam. She would probably agree that you need to go. And don't worry about the money. I'll take care of it. I can probably raise twenty thousand dollars in a week."

"How?"

"I said don't worry about it. They didn't make me the head of this department just because everybody else died off, you know. You just get yourself ready. I think you should leave as soon as finals are over. I'll make the necessary arrangements."

Back at the apartment, Dr. Walker paced nervously back and forth, waiting for his wife to return from her last lab class. As soon as she walked in the door, he started to speak. But she held up her hand. "You caused quite a stir in biochemistry today. Snail slime. That's all anybody talked about all afternoon. I was absolutely trampled by people wanting to know where that stuff came from. You stirred up a regular hornets' nest—then you left!"

"I had to, Janet. I had to get out of there and think. You haven't heard about the telegram. Clyde's in trouble."

"Actually, I have heard about the telegram. After you left, Dr. Atteberry came straight to my office and spilled the whole thing."

Dr. Walker winced. "So what do you think I should do?"

Janet leaned toward her husband and kissed him. "When do you leave, and how long will you be gone?"

Dr. Walker wrapped his arms around his wife and held her a long time.

Chapter 3
MARJAO STATION

Dr. Walker settled back in his seat and tried to relax. He hated flying, but a trip to Africa involved a lot of it, so he tried to think about something else. The flight from Detroit to New York had been crowded and bumpy, but this long flight across the Atlantic to London was much more to his liking. The plane was nearly empty, and he didn't have to share his row.

He went back over the events of the past few days. After he had learned that the slime was from some kind of marine or aquatic animal or maybe a land-based slug or snail, he had gone to the library for some quick brushing up on these kinds of animals. He had hoped to find some clue that would help him identify Clyde's "Burong."

Animals that created this kind of mucus were almost all members of the mollusk family, and most were snails and slugs. But it was hard to conceive of a gastropod that could attack a village. The more he thought about it, the more confusing it became. In his research, he was reminded that there are sea snails that are actually poisonous. It would be plausible that the creatures could live in an inland lake and endanger a village. But even a tremendous migration of the snails would not have been interpreted as an attack. And how could even large sea snails excrete mucus in the amounts involved? Enough that the villagers could collect it and throw it at Clyde's house? It just didn't add up.

Someone at the lab had suggested that they were dealing with some kind of sea monster or sea serpent. Dr. Atteberry had been less skeptical than the other researchers on this topic.

"I've lived long enough and studied long enough to know that we don't know everything," he had said. "Our situation is not that we have learned everything there is to know. It is that we have such limited faculties for understanding. Even when we see the facts, we cannot always distinguish the truth. So I will reserve my judgment on the question of sea monsters. By the way, have any of you ever exhaustively studied the evidence in support of their existence?"

There had been a universal silence on this question. Either no one had or no one wanted to admit it.

So Dr. Walker immediately delved into the material on sea monsters. Of course, he had long had a passing interest in the subject, but he had never had a reason to dig really deep into the evidence. He was astonished to discover how many sightings had been reported by honest and intelligent people. Sea captains, lawyers, doctors, policemen, pilots and even well-respected ministers had reported seeing huge animals that had to be considered "monsters."

Dr. Walker smiled. He had himself, as a young college student, stood on the shores of Loch Ness on a tour of the British Isles, looked into its caramel-colored waters and dreamed of Nessie lolling about on the bottom. In his mind's eye he could see the great beast, perhaps a holdover from some prehistoric age, swimming slowly along the lake's deep bottom in quest of arctic char. The beast moved quickly in spite of its enormous size and raked at the fish with razor-sharp teeth. The char had scrambled away in panic, but Nessie had seized another in its teeth, shaking its head rapidly. The char had all but exploded and then disappeared down the beast's gullet to join its fellows in the giant maw. Nessie had then turned in a long, graceful arc and headed back to its subterranean cave.

Young Samuel Walker had stood entranced and fixated on the unseen depths below, when suddenly a large frog jumped into the water at his feet. Samuel had jumped several feet backwards, expelling his breath in a sound like "Yaawaa!" Then he realized the splash had been nothing but a frog. He had quickly looked around to see if he had been observed, but there was no one around. Samuel had blushed in spite of the fact there were no witnesses, jumped back on his rented bicycle and ridden directly back to the Loch Ness museum in record time.

Dr. Walker laughed at the memory. *My only brush with a sea monster—and it was a frog!*

Three days earlier he had gone in quest of sea monsters in the one place he felt confident in finding them—the library.

He had learned that sea monsters can be placed into several categories. There are the traditional dragonlike sea monsters that reportedly smashed ships and ate sailors, then burned the ships with their breath. When reading about these dragons, he could not help but be reminded of the biblical Leviathan of Job 41. That creature warranted further investigation.

There were the giant squid and the giant octopus, the "kraken" made famous by Norse mythology. They really had attacked and sunk ships.

Then there were sea serpents. These beasts had been reported even in relatively modern times, and they had been seen by as many as a hundred people at once. Some of them had even surfaced in harbors of cities, such as Vancouver, British Columbia and Gloucester, Massachusetts. These serpents had not been sighted just once but many times over a period of years. The evidence for the existence of these marine monsters was overwhelming and irreproachable. And the drawings made of these serpents were consistent in their main features. That there were actually large sea serpents in the ocean seemed to be an indisputable fact.

Then there were the sharks and whales, beasts that had terrified and fascinated man since the beginning of ocean voyages. The tales of their attacks against swimmers and small boats and ships were numerous and, thought Dr. Walker, unnerving. *I have never considered myself a coward, but I hope the Burong is more closely related to the slugs than to the sea monsters. I used to think I was adventurous, but I guess I'm too old to want to find some remnant of the Jurassic Age!*

When the plane took off from London, he pulled out his maps. He would land in Burundi, where he would board a train to the Interior. He was to meet Clyde at a small city in Uganda named Chemechi, then they would travel to the mission station at Marjao. Barring unforeseen delays, he would arrive in Chemechi in four days. That would be February 1. *As soon as I get to Chemechi, I will begin keeping a diary to document everything*

23

that happens, he thought. *Hopefully, it will make for very dull reading.*

When the train pulled into Chemechi, a very tired scientist was met by his old college friend Rev. Clyde Derrington.

"How are you, Sam? And how's Janet?"

"Good to see you, Clyde," replied his friend. "I'm fine, and Janet's terrific. She sends you her love. And she says you are to take good care of me."

"Great. I wish I could see her again. How was your trip?"

"Fine. At least, the first four days of it!"

Rev. Derrington laughed. "It is quite a little jaunt, isn't it?"

"I'll say. And if you think that's a jaunt, I hope you don't tell me that your mission station is just a stone's throw from here."

"Just around the corner," quipped Rev. Derrington. "And I'll be glad to get back."

"How long will it take to get there?"

"Three days, if the weather holds up."

"*Three* days!"

"Well, it takes a while to walk fifty-two miles through the jungle, Sam. But let's not get ahead of ourselves. You need to rest. I've got you a room in the hotel. It's right next to mine. In fact, they have adjoining doors. We'll go eat dinner, and I can fill you in. Then you can sleep tonight. Tomorrow we'll work on our strategy, and we'll leave early the next morning. That'll give you a couple nights to catch up on your rest before we start for the mission."

They met at eight o'clock that night in the hotel restaurant. After ordering, Rev. Derrington brought Sam up-to-date on the happenings at Marjao Station.

"I hardly know where to begin, Sam. I suppose I should start with the very beginning—three years ago when we first established Marjao Station.

"I had been working in Burundi, in the capital city of Bujumbura. The society had sent me there to assist a native pastor who was having some difficulties. After I had been there six years, the church was healthy, and the pastor had been trained. When I felt that church situation was stable, I made my plans to leave. I had been hearing of an unreached tribe west of here. Although some of the men from this tribe had worked in the cities and had probably heard the Gospel, there were no churches in their villages. This I hoped to remedy by starting a mission station and eventually training native pastors.

"The Steven Johnsons, whom I mentioned in my letter, had worked with me in Burundi. Steven is an extremely capable man. He is a wonderful preacher, besides being a terrific handyman. He has basically built our mission station with his own hands, with the assistance of a few native men and his son, Peter. Mrs. Johnson is a nurse, and she has been most useful at the station. Her talents are the ones that have stirred up the most interest among the villagers at Marjao. They were sadly in need of medical attention, and she has been able to help many of them, especially the children.

"Well, when the Johnsons heard that I was planning to start a jungle mission station, they wanted in immediately. I actually tried to discourage them, because I wasn't sure it was the right place for a family. But I was wrong, and I'm glad I didn't refuse them.

"The village of Marjao is pretty much the jumping-off point into the jungle. In fact, it really is past the jumping-off point! There's nothing west of there until you've crossed several hundred miles of jungle.

"When we arrived at Marjao, we set up our tents and began to build wooden houses—huts, really. Steven used the native woods for the frames and built thatched roofs. Within a few days we had very satisfactory living quarters. The Johnsons had a two-room hut, while mine had just one room. They were small, but they really were comfortable. Steven even managed to install a glass window in each hut—complete with screens!

"Within a few weeks, we had convinced the natives to come to our station for Bible studies. They were very interested in our Bibles. A few of the men from the tribe had learned to speak and read English while working in the city, but none of the women or children could read, and only two or three of them could speak English. We have started teaching some of them English, and we have started trying to translate the Bible into their native language."

"Do they have a written language?" asked Dr. Walker.

"They do now," said Rev. Derrington, smiling. "Steven and I worked with the men who could speak English and reduced their dialect to a manageable number of characters. Then we began compiling a lexicon of their language. We have already translated some of the simpler Bible verses into their language. We hope to develop a New Testament within two years."

"That's fantastic!" exclaimed Dr. Walker. "That must be a very gratifying project."

"It is," agreed Rev. Derrington. "But it's also a lot of work! It takes a tremendous amount of time and energy. If Steven were not here, I'm quite sure I couldn't manage it.

"Fourteen months ago we talked to the villagers

about helping us build a chapel. It's actually just a large, open pavilion with a thatched roof. They were excited to help us. They had never built a large building, only small huts. We were able to complete a nice chapel in just a few weeks.

"Then we started to build the infirmary because the Johnsons' hut was too small to house the patients who needed to stay overnight. And I guess Martha got a little tired of having patients in her house all day! Anyway, she asked us to build her an infirmary, and we agreed.

"At first the natives were helpful. They were excited about building something for Martha. They are naturally very expressive, and they wanted to show their appreciation for her care. When they found out she wanted an infirmary, they couldn't wait to get started.

"Then the whole thing began to unravel. I still haven't sorted everything out in my mind. All I know for sure is that things turned sour in a hurry."

Rev. Derrington paused as the waiter came to refill their glasses. He sat quietly until the waiter had passed out of earshot.

"Steven, Peter, Jendel and I were working on the frame of the infirmary one morning when suddenly we heard shouts from the village. In a few minutes one of the village leaders came to the compound and ordered us to leave. We asked him what the trouble was, and he would not answer us. I'm telling you, Sam, the man was terrified—completely panic-stricken. My understanding of their dialect is still imperfect, but I could hardly make sense of anything he said. He was babbling incoherently. I tried to calm him down, but he just waved his arms frantically and shouted that we must go.

"Jendel, who came with me from the church in Burundi, started asking other villagers what had happened. Finally, an old man whom Jendel had befriended told him about the Burong."

"That's where I came in," said Dr. Walker. "Tell me about the Burong."

"At first, we couldn't get any information about the Burong. I told the village leaders firmly that I had no intention of leaving. The people needed to hear the story of Christ, and they needed the infirmary, and I would not leave. When the people heard me say that I would not leave, many of them screamed and cried. I mean, the women of the village went back down the trail weeping and sobbing. The children huddled close to their mothers, looking confused and frightened.

"Eventually we learned that the Burong was some kind of creature. It supposedly lives in a small, deep lake just north of Marjao. This creature had attacked some villagers at a hunting camp some miles north of our village, and several natives were killed. The village leaders at Marjao immediately associated this attack with the building of the infirmary. These people are still superstitious enough to think the two events were connected in some way.

"Then one night I was awakened by loud screaming outside my hut. I wrote you about that, didn't I?"

"Yes, and that's when they threw the slime on your window."

"Right. The men who threw that stuff on my window were dressed up in skins dyed green. They were painted green, and they were wearing yellow feathers in their hair. When I opened the door of my hut to look out, they ran away.

"Well, that is when I contacted you the first time. I was not equipped to explore this Burong question, but I knew you were. In fact, you're the only person I know who is both educated enough and young enough to take on such an investigation."

"Thanks a lot, Clyde. But if you'd asked, I could have given you the names of half a dozen other people!"

Clyde chuckled. "Maybe so, but none of them would have helped me. I knew you would be likely to come. After all, that's what friends are for."

Samuel smiled. "So tell me why you left the mission station."

"Three weeks ago the village was attacked. Several of the villagers' huts were burned to the ground. There was a general panic, and the people fled down the trail past the station. Several were trampled and suffered minor injuries. We took them into the chapel to help them, but as soon as they could walk, they started back down the trail as fast as they could move.

"Here's the really strange part. We could hear an incredible noise coming from the village. It sounded like an elephant screaming, but louder. And then the huts were burning. Peter wanted to run into the village to see what it was, but cooler heads won out, and we stayed where we were.

"In the morning we went to inspect the damage. Three huts had been burned, and about a half acre was scorched. To the north of the village, perhaps twenty trees had been smashed to the ground, and the ground was ripped up like a tractor and plow had been through it!

"Then there were the footprints."

"Footprints?"

"Uh huh. There were huge footprints like those of a...a...well, a dinosaur."

"What?"

"That's right, Sam. I know it sounds crazy, but

there they were. Oh, here, look." With that, he took a small packet from his shirt pocket. "I took pictures. I laid a rifle down beside the tracks for scale."

Dr. Walker grabbed the pictures and took his glasses from his shirt pocket. He carefully examined each picture and said, "Clyde, this is incredible!"

"I know, but it's also true. The tracks led off into the jungle, but within just a few feet they stopped. At least we couldn't find any more. It seemed as if the underbrush was thick enough to keep the prints from being formed, but I don't know—I'm no tracker.

"When the villagers came back, they were really angry. They told us to get out—and they didn't give us any choice. They basically loaded up our stuff on their backs and headed east. About three miles down the trail they put it down. Finally we were able to convince the villagers to carry some of our clothing back to the huts. Then we loaded up our supplies, found some villagers who would come with us, and came here. That's when I sent you the telegram asking you to come."

That night, lying in bed, Dr. Walker tried to sort out the events of the day. What an incredible story! Could it be that there really was some kind of dinosaur out there, just forty miles northwest of where he lay right at this moment? And what about the fire? Were we talking about a dinosaur or a dragon?

One thing was certain—the next few days would be anything but boring. He had started his journal that night before retiring. And it had started off with a bang!

Chapter 4
BURONG

Dr. Walker woke to the sounds of jungle birds and clattering pans. The sun streamed directly into his eyes through the window of the little hut. The young scientist blinked and turned away, then decided he should get up to help his host with breakfast. When he moved, it seemed every single muscle in his body complained, and he groaned as he stiffly rose from his sleeping bag. Three days on the jungle trails plus two nights of sleeping on the ground had left him extremely sore.

He stood and stretched. A catch in his back made him stop. *I've got aches in muscles I didn't even know existed,* he thought. And to make matters worse, he could hear Clyde outside the hut, whistling merrily as he cooked breakfast. *It doesn't seem fair,* he said to himself. Somehow he managed to get dressed.

"Good morning!" said Rev. Derrington as Dr. Walker stepped outside the hut. "Sleep well?"

"Clyde, you are not a nice person," he replied, trying to grin.

Clyde chuckled. "Don't worry about it, Sam. You'll get your trail legs soon enough. You've got a whole month to adjust."

Sam grinned. "Do I get new legs? That'll be great. I've worn these completely out!"

Clyde laughed. "I hope I didn't wake you. I tend to make too much noise in the morning. Peter's complained about it more than once. He's a teenager and needs his sleep—at least that's what he says."

"You know, Clyde, there's a verse in the Bible about that. It says, 'He that blesseth his friend with a loud voice, rising early in the morning, it shall be counted a curse to him.'"

"Yes, Samuel," said Clyde, grinning, "but that only applies to 'early' morning. It's after eight o'clock! I can think of one for you. It says, 'How long wilt thou sleep, O sluggard? when wilt thou arise out of thy sleep?'"

"Okay, Clyde, you win," laughed Dr. Walker. "What's for breakfast?"

"Ham and eggs."

"Ham and eggs? Where did you get ham and eggs?"

"Well, there's a jungle bird here about the size of a chicken," explained the missionary, "and its eggs taste just like chicken eggs."

"Neat. But what about the ham? Do you have jungle hogs too?"

Clyde reached into a wooden box, then pitched a can to Sam. "Nope. Some things you have to bring with you."

Dr. Walker laughed and opened the can of cooked ham. He began to slice the ham and laid it in a griddle on the open campfire.

"What are you planning to do first, Sam?"

"Well, I'd like to see those tracks you were telling me about and the damage done to the jungle and the village, if we can do it without upsetting the villagers."

The missionary nodded his head. "I think we can arrange it. I need to speak to the village elders anyway. I need to tell them we're back and why you're here. They may not like the idea, but it's better to talk to them first rather than letting them find out on their own and come here."

"I think that's wise too. I don't think I want them to get any rougher than they were before."

After breakfast Peter Johnson came over and asked Dr. Walker about his plans. The teenager had taken to the zoologist instantly and had spent every possible moment with him on the trail. Dr. Walker was glad for the young man's company, and he was impressed with his keen mind and strong curiosity.

"I'm going to take a look around the village," Dr. Walker told his young friend. "I want to see if I can figure out what happened the night the village was attacked. Brother Clyde told me you had been to the site. Do you think you could show me around?"

"Yes sir! I'll have to ask my dad, but I'm sure he'll let me go. In fact, he might want to come too."

"I'd be glad if he could come. He knows more about the jungle than I'll ever know, and he might have something to contribute. Would you ask him to join us?"

"I'll be right back!" said Peter, already halfway to his hut.

By noon people from the village had already come to the mission station. They had seen the smoke of the morning fires and were hoping that Mrs. Johnson was among those who had returned. Quite a few had been under her care when she was forced to leave, and they wanted her attention.

After the noon meal Rev. Derrington, Dr. Walker, Mr. Johnson, Peter and Jendel walked into the village. Dr. Walker carried his tiny tape recorder and his camera, along with several other pieces of equipment, in a pack which Peter insisted on carrying for him.

When the men arrived in the village, they found the village elders, who had already anticipated their visit, assembled under a large tree in the center of the community. This was the "formal" meeting place.

"Greetings, friends," said Rev. Derrington in the villagers' native tongue. (Peter interpreted in a whisper for the benefit of Dr. Walker.) "I have returned with a friend. This is Walker."

The head of the council spoke: "Greetings, Derrington. We hoped you would return. We are very glad to have you back here. We were wrong to make you leave. Please do not be angry with us. We were frightened."

"I understand," said the missionary. "Thank you for your kind words. My friend is here to try to help with the Burong."

At the mention of their menace, the villagers murmured. The elder who had spoken frowned. "We will have much trouble if the Burong is disturbed. He has not been here since you left. Can we not just let him alone?"

Dr. Walker noticed that the elder spoke of the Burong as though it were fact. Apparently, this man believed that it did exist!

The missionary placed his hand on Dr. Walker's shoulder. "My friend knows much about these things," he said. "He will not disturb the Burong. But he may help you so that you will not have to be afraid. Please allow him to try to help you. Walker is my friend. I ask you to count him your friend too."

The elder nodded. "Your friend is welcome.

Walker is our guest." Again there was murmuring. The elder stood and looked around, a scowl on his face. "Quiet!" he shouted. "You will be friend to Walker. The missionary Derrington is our friend. Johnson is our friend. And Walker is our friend. You will help him if you can. I say."

The people nodded their heads, then they looked at Walker and smiled. Dr. Walker bowed to them and smiled. They bowed and smiled. The interview was then over, and the villagers walked back to their huts.

Dr. Walker, Peter and Mr. Johnson walked to the west side of the village to inspect the burned huts. Nothing was left except ashes. The people of the village had obviously not visited the huts since the incident. Dr. Walker wondered about that aloud, and Mr. Johnson ventured the opinion that their superstitions had kept them away. "They're probably scared to death to get close. Besides, they had nothing to gain by coming here. Whoever lived here lost everything in the fire, so they did not need to return. By now they have just built new huts."

The ground surrounding the three huts was completely charred and lifeless. Dr. Walker thought it looked like an arson fire started with gasoline or alcohol. Mr. Johnson shrugged his shoulders, saying, "Could have been. These natives have access to gasoline in town. I wouldn't put it past some of them to start the fires just to scare the village and get rid of us."

"But, Mr. Johnson, who would want to get rid of you?" asked Dr. Walker. "After all, your wife is helping the women and children, and even the men need medical attention."

"I know that, and you know that, but she's cutting into the practice of their local medicine man. He absolutely hates us. He once was both the medical and religious leader of the community. Now he's losing ground to Clyde and to my wife, and he's not a bit happy about it. I can see him burning the huts, then saying, 'I told you so!' And many of the villagers—if not most—are still afraid of him."

The men walked to the area north of the village and found the remnants of the tracks. But by this time the incessant rains of the jungle had all but washed them out. The men did find the trees that had been knocked down, and Dr. Walker was amazed at the size of some of them. "What could have knocked these trees down? I mean, unless there really is a beast of tremendous size in the jungle—like the Burong."

"I'm not sure," said Mr. Johnson. "Elephants can do it, but they don't. Elephants are destructive feeders, and they destroy a lot of trees just by ripping the bark off them, but they don't go around knocking them down. Not twenty of them at a time, that's for sure! Besides, there are very few elephants in this area. Most of them live in the savannas far to the north."

"Right," said Dr. Walker. "I spent two years in the savanna around Mt. Kilimanjaro. A great deal of that time I did nothing but track and keep records on a big family of elephants. And I never saw them knock down a tree. I've heard of rogue elephants who would attack a village or knock down a tree. But as you say—twenty trees at once? Not likely."

The scientist continued: "Steven, tell me the truth: do you think there is some kind of creature—this Burong—out here?"

Steven took off his hat and ran his hand through his hair. "Samuel, I have been wondering about that ever since this thing started. It doesn't make sense to me either. But the more I think about it, the more I am inclined to think that maybe there is."

"Dad, you don't mean it!" exclaimed Peter.

"Well, Son, I can't explain the things that have happened in any other way. I'm not saying there definitely is a dragon or a dinosaur or—whatever—but I think there could be. I'm going to stay open-minded about it until we know for sure."

"You know, Steven," said Dr. Walker, "one of my colleagues back at MCU, Dr. Horace Atteberry, said almost the same thing: 'I'm going to reserve my judgment on the question of sea monsters.' After looking at all this, I'm going to have to concur. In fact, I would say it is not only a possibility but a very plausible explanation for the evidence. It sounds farfetched, but I'm going to assume there is a creature, and then try to prove that there isn't!"

That evening Dr. Walker was sitting alone in his hut. Clyde Derrington had joined the Johnsons. Samuel could hear them singing. Mr. Johnson was playing the guitar. With the stillness of the night, the music was lovely. Dr. Walker had turned on his notebook computer and started updating his journal. He recorded his opinion concerning the Burong: "If I prove myself wrong, fine; but if I can't prove anything, everyone who reads this will think I'm crazy!"

Just then there was a tap at the window. Dr. Walker looked up to see Peter. "Come in, Peter. I was just finishing."

"Can I talk to you for a minute?" he asked, opening the door.

"Certainly. What can I do for you?"

"Well, I just wanted... Hey, is that a computer?" asked Peter, sitting down on a campstool beside the professor.

"Yes. Would you like to see it?"

Peter took the computer from Dr. Walker. "Wow! This is light!"

Dr. Walker chuckled. "It was when I left Michigan. After three days on the trail, I was beginning to wonder why I brought it."

"Why *did* you bring it?"

"Well, I am keeping a journal of all these events. I want a record of the discoveries, and I don't want to be prejudiced later. So I am recording the events as they happen and the evidence as we find it. You may also have noticed that I was taking pictures outside the village. I will add those to my journal later."

Peter nodded. "How do you expect to power this thing? I mean, I know it uses batteries, but won't they run out long before you leave here?"

Dr. Walker showed Peter the back of the computer. "This thing uses a rechargeable battery that lasts eight hours. I have two of them, and I charged them both back in town. If I use the computer just twenty or thirty minutes a night, I should be all right. I am just making brief notes. I'll flesh out the journal later. And if the batteries do run out, I have a backup." With that, he pulled a yellow legal pad and three pencils from his backpack.

Peter laughed. "Let's hope it doesn't come to that!"

"Well, we scientists are a brave lot. We will put

up with almost any hardship for the cause of science. By the way, where's the soft drink machine?"

"I know," said Peter, "and no fast food. But, Dr. Walker, there really was something I wanted to talk to you about. I...do you...is it..." Peter stared at the computer awkwardly.

"Do I really think there is a dinosaur here?" Dr. Walker prompted.

"Yes, that's it. Or a monster or something? Do you really think so?"

"That's hard to say, Peter. But I'm going to assume there is until I know there isn't. You see, if I assume there isn't, I won't work nearly as hard or use nearly as much creativity to find it. I'll just put in the work to make a case, then I'll quit. Do you see what I mean?"

"Sure, I understand. By the way, Dr. Walker, I think so too, and I have from the very beginning."

"Really, Peter? What made you think so?"

"Well, for one thing, those natives were really terrified. I mean, you could just say 'Burong,' and the little children would cry. It's as if they have seen the thing. But they won't tell you they have. Of course, they won't say they haven't either. They just won't talk about it.

"For another, when I saw those tracks and the fallen trees and the huts burned out, I couldn't think of any other explanation. These are sensible, mature people here at Marjao. Why would they make up wild stories about a monster if they didn't have some reason to believe it? They wouldn't tell Brother Derrington there was a monster if they didn't think it was true.

"But do such animals exist? I mean, I know there have been sea monsters and there once were dinosaurs—I've seen skeletons of dinosaurs in museums, so I know they're not a hoax. But what about the slime? and the fire? Could an animal do that?"

"Yes, Peter, there have been such animals," said the scientist, fired by the boy's enthusiasm and curiosity. "And some of these abilities still exist in the animal world. The slime, for instance, is excreted by many different kinds of animals. It is just a slick mucus that allows them to move forward with less friction. You've surely seen snails and slugs that leave silvery trails behind them."

"Yes sir, but what about the fire?"

"Have you ever heard of the bombardier beetle?"

"No—at least I don't think so."

"Well, this beetle has two small chambers of chemicals on the tip of its abdomen. When the beetle feels threatened, it forces these two chemicals into a mixing chamber in its body; then it is expelled. The chemicals combine to form a highly corrosive acid. Now I realize that's not fire, but it's pretty close. It is possible that some dinosaurs may have been able to do something along the same lines. Only in their case, the resulting combination of chemicals would have produced a flame."

"You mean, like a fire-breathing dragon?"

"Exactly. We can't prove it, of course, but neither can we disprove it. But it does seem possible. In fact, the Bible even talks about such a beast."

"It does?"

"Yes, it does—in Job 41. It is referred to as the Leviathan. Why don't you read that passage? I think you'll be surprised at the detail in the description. We can talk about it some more tomorrow, if you like."

Peter stood and handed Dr. Walker his computer. "Hmmm. A fire-breathing dragon. Maybe here at Marjao. Wow!"

"Now, Peter, don't get too excited about it, and don't go around telling everybody I said there was a fire-breathing dragon around here. I don't know any such thing, and I didn't say it. You asked me questions, and I answered them as best I could. Don't put two and two together and get five."

Peter grinned. "Okay, Dr. Walker. I won't say anything about it. But I'd really love to help you look for it. And I won't be surprised if we find it!"

"I would be content just to prove that such a creature exists," said Dr. Walker. "I'm not sure I want to find it. At least, not up close and personal!"

Chapter 5
THE BURONGI

On the western shore of Lake Nyvasu, set back in the trees some two hundred yards, lay the hidden mouth of a deep cave. As evening came on and the shadows turned to blackness, smoke poured forth from the cave's mouth. A shrill shriek filled the night sky, and the sound of pulsating drums could be heard from deep within the cave's belly.

A hundred feet or more underground, some quarter of a mile from the cave's mouth, a band of green-painted natives huddled before a stone altar. The drummers kept up a steady rhythm, while the bodies of the worshipers swayed like the waves of the lake. Two natives added wood to the fire of the altar while another fanned it with a woven mat until the coals grew white-hot.

The altar was in the form of a great beast. Its belly was open and filled with the hot coals; the chimney curved upward thirty feet, forming a long, serpentine neck. Atop the neck was the head of a dragon, with hollow eyes and flared nostrils;

stone teeth filled the great gaping mouth. The entire altar had been carved from the wall of the cave, and its head reached the ceiling of the cathedral-like chamber. Smoke billowed from the dragon's eyes, nose and mouth and curled upward through crevices in the chamber roof to escape through the top of the cave.

The worshipers began to chant, at first just a low, rhythmic humming. As the chant progressed, it became louder and took the form of a prayer song or ballad to the Burong.

These were the Burongi—the people of the Burong. They were the dragon-worshipers—keepers of the Burong yet servants. Their tradition was as old as memory, and their religion was their life. They lived to serve the Burong and to protect it from intrusion.

As the chanting grew louder, a trumpet was blown. This trumpet was formed from the horn of the most feared animal in Africa, the cape buffalo. It had been taken by skill in hunting, and its blast represented the strength of both the men and the animals of the jungle.

Suddenly all was still. A lone figure came from the shadows and stood before the altar, bathed in its eerie light. This was Aja, priest of the Burongi. He was dressed in a spectacular costume, representing the Burong itself. Aja's chest was covered with the undershell of a great land tortoise; his cape was of crocodile skin. His legs were covered with the skin of a great constrictor, and that same serpent's head served as a mask and headdress. Above the mask, with its gaping mouth and horrible teeth, a fringe of yellow feathers formed a gaudy frill. Aja was terrifying in his costume, and the Burongi trembled before him. In their minds, at that moment, Aja was the Burong.

Aja raised his arms, and the men beside the altar forced air into the coals with a makeshift bellows, forcing flames to the top of the altar's terrible figure. The flames lit the creature's eyes and sent sparks showering from its mouth and nose onto the cowering natives below. Another blast of air shot flames from the dragon's mouth. The trumpet was blown again, sending a great quake through the audience.

This was repeated again and again and again.

Finally all was still. Aja spoke. "We are the Burongi."

The natives repeated, "We are the Burongi!"

"Keeper of the Burong."

"We are his servants."

"We are the people..."

"Of the Burong."

"The Burongi."

"The Burongi."

Aja held up his hand for silence. "All is not well. White men camp only two days from here. They build new buildings. They mean to stay. We chased them away, but now they have returned. We must make them leave. If we let them stay, they will bring others who will find the Burong. We cannot kill them. If we kill them, others will come. We must make the white men leave."

"We will do as you command," was the answer. "We are the Burongi."

Suddenly this scene was interrupted by the sound of steps along the cave's floor. Aja was angered by this interruption. Who would dare enter while Aja stood before the altar?

Into the light darted a young runner. He was breathless and exhausted, but he struggled to maintain his composure. He was in the presence of Aja, Sacred Keeper of the Burong. He fell at Aja's feet.

"You have brought news?"

The young man nodded his head but did not answer. A spasm racked his body. He coughed.

Aja touched the young man's shoulder and bid him rise. The young runner stood to his feet.

"Speak."

"White men come!"

"How many?"

"Three."

"Where are they now?"

"One day away. They are camped by the falls of the river. They are coming to Nyvasu, I am sure. They will be here late tomorrow."

Aja looked shaken by this news. The audience held its breath collectively to see how their Sacred Keeper would react.

"We must not let them come," Aja said at last. "But we must not let them know we are here. I must meet with the Sacred Council at once. We must make plans. Burongi, to your homes!"

"Sacred Keeper, we obey!"

Chapter 6
NYVASU MWERI

Two days of hard traveling had put Dr. Walker's party about sixteen miles northeast of the mission station. Everything had gone reasonably well—so far. They had faced no opposition from the village about traveling up the trail to Lake Nyvasu.

Dr. Walker was accompanied by Steven Johnson, Peter and several native bearers. Clyde Derrington had felt compelled to remain at the mission station for the sake of relations with the villagers and for the safety of Mrs. Johnson.

Just after breakfast Dr. Walker jotted down a few notes on his yellow pad. When he had finished, he called to Mr. Johnson. "Steven, could I talk to you for a minute before we get back on the trail?"

"Sure, Sam." He laid down the pack he had been arranging.

"Steven, are you sure we're on the right trail?"

"As sure as I can be. The men of the village pointed out this trail as the one to Lake Nyvasu. They said it was about two days' travel, but, Sam, they travel faster than we do."

Dr. Walker chuckled. "That's not hard to believe. Those four villagers you hired to carry our things have been loaded down, and they still manage to keep up. I'm sure if they weren't behind me, I'd still be dragging into camp. Considering they're each carrying sixty pounds, I'd be embarrassed to have them pass me up."

Now it was Steven's turn to chuckle. "I think you're doing great. First you walked the fifty-two miles to the mission station; now you've hiked the sixteen or so miles we've traveled in the past two days. And you're not exactly used to this kind of travel."

"Or the heat! It was about ten degrees when I left Michigan. It must be ninety-five out here during the day."

"At least, and the humidity is well over ninety percent!"

"Well, at least there is shade," said Dr. Walker. "How far do you think we still have to travel?"

"About seven miles, I think. That should put us on the southern shore. And I don't see how we could have missed the right trail, since there haven't been any forks in it. Just a straight shot through the jungle. I sent Peter back down the trail to call the bearers. We need to be on our way before it starts getting hot again."

"All right, Steven. I think I have everything packed. It will take me less than five minutes to be ready."

Suddenly the two men were startled to hear Peter's voice calling from back down the trail. "Dad! Dad! The bearers are gone!"

Mr. Johnson sprinted past Dr. Walker who was right on his heels. In a few seconds they reached the spot where the bearers had camped. Peter was standing in the middle of their campsite. The fire pit was just cold ashes, and the equipment and packs the bearers had carried were neatly stacked beneath a tarp. There was no sign of any of the four villagers.

"That's great," said Mr. Johnson. "I can't believe they just left."

Dr. Walker pulled the tarp off the packs and said, "I'll need some of this stuff when we get to the lake. We'll just have to divide it up among the three of us as best we can."

"Right," agreed Mr. Johnson. "Peter and I will lighten our packs, and you tell us what we need to carry. We can leave the food packs here. I'll just make a sling for them to keep them off the ground. The ants would devour everything if we left the packs where they are. We can pick up what we need for our return trip when we start back from the lake."

Peter stood there staring at the two men. Finally Mr. Johnson noticed his expression. He raised an eyebrow as if to say, *What are you looking at?*

"Aren't you mad at those villagers?" he asked. "I can't believe you're so calm about this!"

Mr. Johnson smiled and placed his hand on his son's shoulder. "Peter, I'm not angry with those fellows. In fact, I really expected them to leave before this. You know how frightened they were of the Burong. None of the villagers have been to Nyvasu in years. The thought of being just a day away from the lake must have scared them to death. I noticed their nervousness yesterday on the trail, and they were very quiet last night. I'm just glad they left our supplies here. I was concerned that they might just turn around and carry off everything."

Dr. Walker nodded. "I thought they were leaving too. They kept stealing glances at each other when we made camp. I made sure to get the absolute essentials for our investigation from them last night. I kept them with me. But I am glad they left the rest of this stuff as well."

Peter shrugged his shoulders. "Show me what

you want me to carry. I'm ready to go. We won't find the Burong if we don't get started."

Dr. Walker grinned at Mr. Johnson, who winked at him. Peter seemed to be the most enthusiastic member of this little expedition. The two men wanted to find evidence of the Burong's existence, but Peter actually wanted to find the Burong!

Within thirty minutes the now smaller party was back on the trail. Peter led, hacking away the undergrowth. Mr. Johnson followed but kept immediately behind Peter to help him find the way. Periodically he made notations on his makeshift map as they progressed. Dr. Walker brought up the rear. He was determined to keep up. By noon, they had traveled nearly six miles.

"Shouldn't be much farther now," said Mr. Johnson. "Before we left, one of the villagers who has been here told me we should cross a small stream just before we see the lake. The jungle has gotten thicker in the last few hundred yards, so I expect to see that stream pretty soon. We'll take just a short break to eat; then we'll try to get to the lakeshore before it gets dark."

Dr. Walker dropped his pack and lay back against it. His back was hurting, and his legs felt like rubber. Finally he got up and started to reach into his pack for something to eat. As he was rummaging around in his pack, he heard a branch

break in a tree above him. He looked up just as a large snake fell out of the tree and onto the ground beside him. Dr. Walker froze. He stared at the snake, which was raising its head from the ground to stare back at him. He whispered hoarsely to his friend, "Steven. Steven, hey!"

Dr. Walker never took his eyes from the snake as he tried to take a step backwards. When he moved his foot, the snake swayed toward him menacingly. He froze again. He heard a metallic click from behind him, then a terrific boom. The snake's head had exploded.

Dr. Walker sat down.

Mr. Johnson walked over to the snake, picked it up, took out his hunting knife and skinned it expertly.

"What...what are you doing?" asked Dr. Walker, still shaking.

Grinning, Mr. Johnson replied, "I thought you might like to have this, so I'll just tack it to a tree, and by the time we get back, it will be pretty well cured." He sat down and began cleaning the inside of the skin.

Peter walked over and handed Dr. Walker a drink of water. "You all right?" he asked.

"I...I think so." The scientist was a little embarrassed. "I've been studying snakes for years; you'd think I'd get used to them."

"Well, I doubt you've ever had one delivered to you just like that before," said Peter. "Airmail, I mean!"

Dr. Walker laughed, but Mr. Johnson was very serious when he asked, "Where did the snake come from?"

Dr. Walker thought for a moment, then answered, "I think it fell out of that tree," looking up and pointing at the broken branch.

Then Mr. Johnson's question triggered something in the scientist's mind. "Steven," he asked, "are you thinking what I'm thinking?"

"Yes, Sam. That snake was a Gaboon viper; they don't climb trees."

Peter looked confused. "But if they don't climb trees, where...?" He left the question unfinished.

"I'm not sure what it means," said Mr. Johnson, "but I think somebody doesn't want us to get to Nyvasu. Sam, did Clyde tell you about the men who threw that slime on his hut?"

"He told me something about it. Let's see, he said that he hadn't seen them before and that they wore strange costumes; that they were painted green and had yellow feathers in their hair. Do you think—"

"I don't know, but let's keep our eyes open," said Mr. Johnson. "Somebody obviously doesn't want us to get to Nyvasu. And it could be them. So let's

be careful. Peter, you follow me. Doctor, you bring up the rear and keep an eye on the trail behind."

The men cut their lunchtime short and started down the trail once more. They moved as quickly as they could while still maintaining their vigilance. Within an hour they were standing on the south shore of the lake.

While the Johnsons set up camp, Dr. Walker took a short stroll along the water's edge. He was not investigating now, just looking. So this was Nyvasu Mweri or Lake Nyvasu. It wasn't very impressive. From his vantage point some twenty feet above the lake's surface, he could see the opposite shore. He estimated that the lake was less than six miles long and no wider than a mile at any point. It curved away to the left along the valley floor. He could not see the end of the lake since it curved out of sight, but he could not imagine that this extension was very long. The valley was too steep north to south for that extension to be anything more than just a short addition to the main lake. Two small islands dotted the southern part of the lake.

Dr. Walker raised his binoculars and scanned the shore. He could see nothing of settlements. In fact, it looked as though no one had ever stood by this lake before. He could not imagine a more tranquil scene. A feeling of great peace came over him as he stood watching the small waves of the

lake lap against the large rock which he had made his outpost.

Suddenly, his reverie was broken by a shout from Peter. "Doctor! Come quick!"

Dr. Walker climbed down from his rock and ran toward the camp. Peter appeared on the trail. "There you are! Come quick! The jungle's on fire!"

Peter led the way with Dr. Walker following close on his heels. Mr. Johnson, who had been stowing the gear, shouted, "We're going to have to move quickly! The fire is moving this way. The fire is coming from the west, so we'll head east. If worse comes to worst, we'll dump everything in the lake."

"But some of my equipment will be ruined if it gets wet," protested Dr. Walker.

"Wet or burned, Sam—take your choice. But it may not come to that. Peter, hurry! Get your pack and start down the trail to the right."

"Yes sir!"

Dr. Walker seemed to be all thumbs. Still it took him no more than five minutes to put his things together and follow Steven Johnson down the trail. When he reached his previous perch at the water's edge, a new thought came to him. He quickly took his canvas tarp down to the water and soaked it. Then he wrapped his equipment bag in the wet canvas and placed it on top of the large,

flat rock. Soon he was running on down the trail.

The fire passed by to the south. The party of three didn't find it necessary to get wet after all. Backtracking, they picked up Dr. Walker's equipment, still safely intact. "That's a relief," said Dr. Walker. "I would've been severely handicapped in my investigation if I'd lost this equipment. Say, Steven, aren't fires rare in the jungle?"

"They are this time of the year," he answered, standing on the rock and scanning the western shore with Samuel's binoculars. "It hasn't really dried out yet. Sometimes, in the late summer, lightning starts fires. But there hasn't been a thunderstorm today."

"Then what do you suppose—"

"You mean '*who* do you suppose,' don't you?" asked Mr. Johnson, looking down at the young scientist. "That fire was deliberately set."

"How do you know?"

"Sam, you understand logic. If you eliminate causes that are not possible, you arrive at the one that is. That last possibility, however unlikely, is the cause. Now, what are the usual possibilities?"

Dr. Walker thought for a moment: *lightning, electricity, accident and arson*. Then, after a moment he said, "I see your point."

Peter spoke up. "No lightning and no electricity out here. So someone must have started the

fire—either by accident or on purpose."

Mr. Johnson looked at his son. "Have you ever known a native to start an accidental fire in the jungle?"

Peter shook his head. "No sir. In fact, Rev. Derrington says the natives are extremely careful with fire. He's never even heard of an accidental fire in the jungle. So that leaves arson. Do you mean someone out here started that fire?"

"That seems to be it," said his dad. "Someone is trying to scare us off. Two impossible accidents in one day are a little hard to swallow."

"There could be one other possibility," said Dr. Walker, looking out at the lake.

"What's that?" asked Mr. Johnson.

"The Burong."

Father and son looked at each other. They couldn't argue that point.

Dr. Walker looked up. "Well?"

"It is a possibility," admitted Mr. Johnson. "At least, judging from what happened back at Marjao. Something torched those huts, that's for sure. And whatever it is, it's capable of producing a really hot flame. Jungles don't burn all that easily except in the dry season. This time of year the undergrowth never dries out."

"Well, whatever it is, man or beast, I'm not

letting it scare me away from this investigation," said Dr. Walker, standing to his feet. "I've come way too far to turn back now."

Chapter 7
POSSIBILITIES

That night the men set up just one tent and kept a watch all night in two-hour shifts. Even Peter took his turn. None of them slept well, in spite of their weariness.

In the morning they took a careful inventory of the supplies and equipment and discovered that in their haste they had left behind one of the food packs which had contained their sugar, coffee and freeze-dried foods. They mourned it briefly but decided not to attempt to retrieve it.

"We need to be getting on with the investigation," said Dr. Walker, and both the Johnsons agreed.

"I suppose we are going up the east side of the lake," offered Peter.

"Yes," said Dr. Walker, "I think that's as good a place as any to start."

"Exactly what will we be looking for?" asked Peter.

"We need to look for tangible evidence of the Burong's existence, for one. And we need to see if we can locate the natives with the green and yellow costumes. They seem to be behind a lot of the events of the past few weeks. In fact, I'd be more likely at this point to blame them than to believe some lake-dwelling creature has suddenly come out of hiding."

"My thoughts exactly," agreed Mr. Johnson. "Apparently our work at the mission station is perceived as a threat to them in some way. My guess is, this group is some kind of cult religion, and they are therefore natural enemies of the Gospel and the work of God. They had probably hoped we would have left by now, but when they saw us starting another building, they decided to act."

"So now you're saying there isn't any Burong?" asked Peter.

"No, Peter," answered his father. "It's still possible there is some kind of creature here. In fact, I'm just guessing, but it wouldn't surprise me if he was, in some way, the focus of their religion."

"Good point," agreed Dr. Walker. "He could be a god to them. And that in itself may lend evidence to the Burong's existence, rather than making its existence less likely."

"So what exactly should I look for?" asked Peter.

Mr. Johnson looked to the scientist for the answer to that question.

"Well, Peter, a large animal that lived in the water would have some place it preferred for getting in and out. It would look like a muddy slide."

"You mean like hippos or crocodiles would make?"

"Exactly—but the ground was pretty torn up around the village," continued Dr. Walker. "If the Burong was actually there, I'd say its underside is rough, not smooth. Hippos and crocs are smooth underneath, and they smooth out the mud. This animal would tear it up like a plow.

"Also, look for slime. We didn't find any at Marjao, but the villagers associated the slime with the creature. If there is any, it's probably up on the trail. And that brings up a point I've been curious about, Steven," said Dr. Walker, turning to Mr. Johnson. "How do you suppose the Burong got to the village if it didn't use the trail?"

"Does seem odd, doesn't it? We sure didn't see any evidence on the trail that suggested he had used it. For one thing, the trees were all still standing!"

"If there really is a Burong," said Peter, "I think he could make his own trail!"

"So what do you think, Peter?" asked Dr. Walker. "Is he here or isn't he?"

"I don't know, but I'm ready to go find out."

"I thought you might be," said Dr. Walker, grinning. "Lead on, Great White Hunter."

Peter grinned back, scrambled to his feet and shouldered his pack. Soon he was well in the lead along the trail which led around the east side of the lake.

After two miles, the trail suddenly turned to the left and down to the waterline. There it stopped abruptly at a campsite. "Dad! Dr. Walker!" called Peter from the camp. "This seems to be some kind of fishing camp. But the trail stops here!"

The men slid down the bank to join Peter. They scanned the shoreline toward the east. "Nothing but a sheer rock wall all the way down," said Mr. Johnson. "What do you think, Sam?"

Dr. Walker considered the situation momentarily. "I think we should build a raft," he suggested. "These trees should float well enough, and we have lots of nylon cord to tie them together. We can continue along the shore."

"Good idea," agreed Mr. Johnson. "If you men will start cutting down some of the smaller trees, I'll get started on some paddles and a rudder. If the water's not too deep, we can pole the raft along the shore. But the way these rock walls come straight down to the water's edge, I'd say it's pretty deep all along."

Three hours of hard work found the men in possession of a serviceable raft. It had a rudder, two oars fitted into locks, and three poles. The craft floated high in the water and was extremely stable. Mr. Johnson had supervised its construction and had even managed to pitch the smaller tent on the rudder end. It served as a shade and a break from possible rainstorms, and the raft could be steered from inside it.

The men ate a quick lunch of canned luncheon meat, crackers and canned peaches; then they were on their way.

They soon discovered that Mr. Johnson's assessment of the situation was correct. The water was too deep for poling the raft. The poles were not abandoned, however, for the men knew they would be useful later on. For the present, it was necessary to use the makeshift oars.

"How deep is this lake, Dad?" asked Peter. "If it drops off this quickly, do you suppose it's very deep?"

"I'm not sure, Pete. It's not a very large lake, but the lakes in this valley can be extremely deep. This is the southern end, as you know, of the Great Rift Valley, which stretches from way up north at the Dead Sea all the way down here. Lake Tanganyika, the largest of the lakes in the valley, is one of the deepest lakes in the world. Do you remember, Sam, how deep it is?"

73

"Yes, as a matter of fact, I do," answered Dr. Walker. "When I was there working, I remember the game warden telling me it was over 1,700 feet deep at its deepest point. I doubt if this lake's anywhere near that deep, but it might be six or seven hundred feet deep, at any rate."

Peter whistled. "That's hard to imagine. It doesn't even look that far across!"

Mr. Johnson nodded his head. "It's probably a mile across at least, but you're right: this high wall makes it look really narrow."

Dr. Walker was staring across the lake at the western shore.

"What do you see, Sam?" asked Mr. Johnson, shading his eyes and turning his gaze to the west.

"Nothing, really. I was just thinking. With this high wall on the east side, any creature as big as the Burong would have to get out of the water somewhere else on the lake. We've been all along the lake on this side, and we didn't see anything promising. I think we should cross the lake and start working the other side."

"It's getting late," said Mr. Johnson. "I don't think we'd get much done before dark. But I think you're right about crossing. We can't get up this wall to make camp, and I'm not crazy about the idea of trying to camp on the raft. Let's go across now and find a campsite. Tomorrow we can figure

out exactly what to do next."

Peter took the tiller from his dad, and the two men each worked an oar. Within the hour, the raft bumped against the western shore of the lake. Camp was set up. Mr. Johnson built a fire and prepared the meal. Peter found a spring, and after adding some chemicals to the water to make it safe to drink, dinner was served—canned luncheon meat (fried), crackers and canned peaches. The men joked about the limited menu, thanked the Lord for the food and ate heartily.

After dinner, Mr. Johnson and Peter walked down the trail to the north of the campsite. Dr. Walker sat in camp and worked on his journal. He was disappointed with the day's activities. He had discovered nothing significant, but, he admitted, he had eliminated some possibilities. The creature, if it existed, was not using the east side of the lake. In one day he had eliminated half the search. So, while not exactly thrilling, the day had been useful.

When the Johnsons returned, Peter sat down beside Dr. Walker at the campfire. The day had been hot, and it was still stifling, but the small fire provided light. Dr. Walker noticed that Peter had something on his mind but was hesitant to speak of it. "A penny for your thoughts," said the young scientist.

Peter looked up, surprised. "Uh, well, I...you

know, Dr. Walker," he began, "the other day we were talking about the Burong. You said that it could be something like the Leviathan talked about in the Book of Job. Do you still think so?"

Mr. Johnson had walked up and found a place across from the others. He placed a pack behind him and leaned against it. He was evidently interested in the topic of the conversation as well. Dr. Walker shifted uneasily. "Well, I don't think we have conclusive evidence that the Burong even exists. But if it does, yes, I think it could be something like the Leviathan of Scripture. By the way, Peter, did you read through Job 41?"

Peter nodded. "Yes sir, I did, and it seems to fit. Doesn't it?"

Dr. Walker nodded. "Steven, what do you think?"

Mr. Johnson leaned forward, threw a small stick into the fire, then said, "Could be. When I was in Bible college, I studied the Book of Job in a class called Poetical Books. The professor read the descriptions of the Behemoth and the Leviathan in Job 40 and 41. He told us that most Bible scholars consider these passages to be just artistic descriptions of the elephant and the crocodile. You know, 'poetic license' and all that. But there are too many inconsistencies for me to believe that. For instance, Job 40 says the Behemoth had a tail like a cedar. That is definitely not an accurate description of an elephant's tail!"

Dr. Walker laughed. "Right!" he agreed. "An elephant's trunk, maybe, but not its tail!"

"And the crocodile doesn't breathe fire either," added Peter.

"That's right, Son," said Mr. Johnson, "so I concluded that *most Bible scholars,* if that's what they believed, didn't know what they were talking about. Then I read somewhere the theory that these two animals represented the two basic kinds of dinosaurs. The Behemoth represented the plant-eating dinosaurs, such as the brontosaurus, and the Leviathan represented the meat-eating dinosaurs, like tyrannosaurus rex."

"That is one of the classical views of these passages," said Dr. Walker, "but I disagree. I think these were real, living beasts that God described. And the interesting thing is, He speaks to Job as though Job should have been familiar with them. Job didn't seem confused by the descriptions, so he must have heard of the animals before. In fact, he might have even seen them."

Peter, looking intently into the fire, asked, "So what happened to them?"

"Nobody knows for sure what happened to the dinosaurs," answered Dr. Walker. "I personally believe that after the Great Flood of Noah's day, the plant eaters, being unable to adjust to the earth's new climate, starved to death because of the scant vegetation in the new world. And the meat eaters would have starved without large prey animals such as the plant-eating dinosaurs. They would never have been able to catch the smaller animals."

"But if there were no dinosaurs after the Flood," asked Peter, "how would Job have known about them?"

"That's a good question, Peter. You're really thinking. I can think of only two possibilities. One is that the dinosaurs didn't die off immediately after the Flood but over a period of several hundred years. You remember that Nimrod, in the Bible, lived after the Flood. He was considered a 'mighty hunter.' It may be that he gained his reputation and rose to leadership because he protected the people from dangerous dinosaurs. Of course, that's just speculation on my part.

"The Book of Job is one of the really ancient books of the Bible, and it may be that Job lived just after the Flood. So he may have been familiar with dinosaurs.

"Another possibility is that Job actually lived before the Flood. We really don't know where he fit into the biblical chronology. But in any case, he did seem to know about Behemoth and Leviathan."

"Is it possible, Dr. Walker, that the dinosaurs

died off more slowly in unsettled areas?" asked Mr. Johnson. "For instance, after the Flood, people would not have lived here in southern Africa for a long time, or in North America. Do you think Job could have just heard of dinosaurs from the trade that took place around the Mediterranean?"

"That's a good possibility," said Dr. Walker. "I would assume that Job lived in the ancient land of Mesopotamia, around the fertile crescent. That was where Noah lived and apparently most of the godly men before Abraham. If Job lived before Abraham, that's where he would have lived. Mesopotamia did trade with Africa. In fact, you may recall that the nation of Israel, many years later, traded with southern Africa. This trade was one of the primary sources of Solomon's wealth. The trade route could have come straight up the Great Rift Valley, from as far south as present-day South Africa. So any stories of the Leviathan, or of the Behemoth for that matter, could have come from here. Is that what you were getting at?"

"Yes," said Mr. Johnson. "I have been considering that perhaps Job knew about the Leviathan because traders from Africa brought the stories to the Middle East."

"I think that's possible," said Dr. Walker. "Of course, we don't have to explain how God knew about it!"

Peter laughed. "I wish I could get Him to explain

a little more about it. I'm dying of curiosity!"

"And we're going to be dying of exhaustion if we don't get some sleep," said Mr. Johnson. "Let's turn in. I have a feeling tomorrow is going to be a very long day."

Chapter 8
DISCOVERY

High on a bluff overlooking the lake's western shore, three men watched the Walker party making their preparations for the night. The white men prepared their camp on the shore, cutting away the lush grass and laying out their ground cloths. They set up their remaining tent and placed their gear inside. The younger man and the youth went to bed inside. The big man settled himself on the raft. He would take the first watch.

Aja spoke softly: "These men seem to know no fear. They did not stop when we took their bearers. They did not stop when the serpent threatened them. They did not stop when the jungle burned. They seem determined, and I am afraid they are looking for the Burong."

"The big man seems very brave," said Ruma, the oldest of the trio. "He was not afraid of the snake."

"And he always seems to know what to do," said the third. "He makes good choices."

"I have heard of this man from the villagers,"

said Aja. "He is Johnson, and the men there say he can do anything. But it is the other man who worries me. He has a certain calmness about him. And he wants to find out what is here. That is what worries me most—his desire to find out. I believe it will be a problem to us."

"What will we do?" asked the third man.

"We will hide," said Aja. "I do not think we have been seen. We will continue to watch the men, but they must not see us. If they do not find the Burong and if they do not find us, they will leave. They cannot stay long. They do not have much food."

"What about the cave?"

Aja nodded. "We must hide the entrance of the cave. It is far back from the trail. They are looking only along the lake. If they do not find the cave, they will go away after tomorrow.

"Ruma, you will go to hide the entrance to the cave. Be sure of your work. And be silent. You must not be seen. Hurry now before the moon rises. It is darkest now."

As Ruma rose to leave, Aja grabbed his arm. "Hear what I say," he said with a menacing stare. "You must not be seen or heard."

Ruma nodded and moved away.

* * * * *

When Mr. Johnson woke Dr. Walker for his

shift, the young scientist took his place on the raft. He had actually been looking forward to his watch. He was anxious to test a piece of equipment he had brought along, and this was the perfect place for it. He reached into his equipment bag and pulled out a small, unbreakable plastic case. From inside it he took a night-vision telescope. This telescope had the ability to magnify existing light 30,000 times and had 100-power magnification. With this telescope, he was sure he could make out individual objects in the dark on the other side of the lake. From the raft he could also scan the shoreline on this side of the lake. He would spend his two-hour shift watching for... What did he hope to see? The Burong? He smiled a wry smile. If he were going to see the dragon, or sea monster, or whatever it was, a telescope was not a bad way to do it!

He turned the switch that powered up the light magnification unit and extended the tripod's legs. Placing the telescope on his pack he found a semi-comfortable position. As he looked through the viewfinder, he could see the jungle, almost as bright as if it were in daylight, except it was emerald green. The light magnification unit gave everything a bright green cast.

He began his search along the southern end of the lake where he and the Johnsons had first reached the shore. He worked slowly and methodically around the east side of the lake. When he reached the cliffs, he scanned along the bottom where it reached the water. Then he scanned the top of the cliff. This they had not been able to see from the water. There was nothing up there but the jungle.

When he reached the north end of the lake after a half hour of searching, he sat up. His neck was aching and his back was tired. He stood carefully and stretched. Then he moved his pack to a new position, resumed his half-reclining position and started back at the south end of the lake. He scanned along the southern shore, still finding nothing. Then he worked his way up the western shore as well as he could, but he was in an unsatisfactory angle from which to view the whole shore. He needed a position farther out in the lake—perhaps on one of the islands near the south end—but he decided to do that tomorrow night.

He turned around and scanned the western shore north of his position, but he did not see anything out of the ordinary. The small bend of the lake at the north end was out of view, but Dr. Walker didn't think that area was very promising anyway. It was also a deep cut and had sheer walls like the east shore, which made it an unlikely spot for the Burong and for the natives.

Unsuccessful in his search, Dr. Walker stood once more and stretched. *That took just about an hour, and I have time to do it again. But first,* he

said to himself, *I'll look at the bluffs overlooking this side of the shore. I really didn't concentrate on them.*

He resumed his searching position and started back at the south end, following the line of trees silhouetted against the night sky. Every few feet there was a break in the trees, and the face of the bluff shone white against the dark of the jungle. Suddenly his attention was drawn to two dark spots on top of one of the bluffs. Were they trees? No, they were too small to be trees. What then? animals of some kind? As he watched, he was startled when one of them moved. He blinked and looked away from the telescope. Then he looked again. No, they were still. But wait! Now they were farther apart than before. He was sure of it.

He carefully turned the focusing knob, zoomed in to the telescope's limit, then focused again. The two dots were now larger and sharper. That they were not part of the bluff he was now certain. Then the one on the left moved again. It half rose.

Dr. Walker caught his breath—it was a man! He quickly resumed his scan of the bluff, knowing that if he kept the telescope on the two men, they would know they had been discovered. *Better to let them think they haven't been seen,* he reasoned, *or they might leave.*

"Dr. Walker," said a voice from the dark. Dr. Walker jumped.

"Oh, Peter, it's you!"

"I'm sorry I startled you."

"It's okay. I was just thinking and didn't hear you come up."

"What are you doing? What's that?" Peter asked.

"It's a night-vision telescope. I've been scanning the shorelines and the bluffs."

"Can you really see in the dark with it?" asked Peter, getting excited.

"Yes. It magnifies light 30,000 times."

"Did you see anything?"

"I saw two men up there on that bluff behind us—no, don't look. They're still up there."

"What are they doing?" asked Peter without turning around.

"They're just watching us." Then, seeing Peter's eyes travel back to the telescope, he added, "Would you like to try it?"

"Sure!"

Dr. Walker moved the pack and turned the telescope around so Peter could reach it. "Look over there toward the two islands. You'll have to look around at a lower magnification power to find them, then zoom in. You should then be able to focus and make out individual trees."

Peter looked through the telescope and soon found the islands. With Dr. Walker's help, he made the proper adjustments. "Man, this is great! It's just like daytime!" Then he sat up. "Are you going back to bed?" he asked.

"Yes, I'd better get some sleep."

"Can I—can I use this, or do you want to put it away?"

"Well, go ahead and use it," said Dr. Walker, "but please be careful with it. It belongs to a friend of mine—and he's a friend I'd like to keep! And, by the way, don't get too curious about those fellows up on the cliff. If you spend too much time trying to find them, they'll leave."

In the morning Dr. Walker woke to the smell of sizzling meat. It smelled good until he realized it was canned luncheon meat. *Well,* he thought to himself, *it's edible—barely.* He dressed and joined his friends at the fire.

"Good morning, Sam," greeted Mr. Johnson good-naturedly. "That's some telescope you've got."

"Oh, did you use it too?"

"Of course! Never could resist a new toy. And that is a neat one! Peter didn't want to go to bed after his watch, and I never thought anything could keep him awake all night."

Peter laughed. "The truth is, Dad just wanted me out of his way so he could use it!"

Dr. Walker chuckled. "I had never used one before last night. And yes, Peter, it is pretty neat.

One of my friends, a hunter, uses it to locate big game before the sun comes up. By the way, where is it?"

"I put it back in the case," replied Mr. Johnson. "I didn't want it to get damaged."

"Thanks," said Dr. Walker. "Like I said, my friend is a hunter. You never want to upset a guy who owns forty guns!"

It was Mr. Johnson's turn to laugh. Then he changed the subject. "Your friends on the bluff left before sunup. I guess they thought we'd see them when it got light. They didn't know that with your telescope it's never dark out here!"

Dr. Walker looked up at the bluff. It was farther than he had thought. It was just possible that the natives would not have seen them looking up at the bluff with the telescope, but he had been right to use caution. He turned his attention back to his friends. "We need to search this shore today. Have you got any suggestions?"

Mr. Johnson spoke up. "We need to keep the raft, and we need to follow the trail. I think we're going to have to split up."

Dr. Walker shook his head. "No, we need to stay together. I don't think it would be safe to get separated."

"I've been thinking about it," replied Mr. Johnson. "Let me explain; then if you still don't want to do it, fine. We'll think of something else.

"I think you or I should stay on the raft and stay abreast of the other two on the trail. We can keep in communication at all times. The trail probably runs close to the lake all the way down. When we've traveled about half the way, we'll trade off. That way neither of us has to walk all the time."

"Peter or one of us would have to take the trail alone," said Dr. Walker.

"I don't mind walking alone," Mr. Johnson responded. "I'll take the first shift on the raft. Then when you and Peter get tired, I'll take the shore. We may have to switch off more than once anyway."

Dr. Walker thought it over. Then his face brightened. "Why didn't I think of this before?" he said, hurrying to his pack. When he returned, he was carrying two small headsets, each connected to a small radio. "These belong to another friend of mine, a balloonist, and he uses them to communicate with his chase team."

"Two-way radios?" asked Peter.

"Yes, FM radios, to be exact," said Dr. Walker.

"You've got cool friends!" Peter commented.

"One of the fringe benefits of working in a science department," said Dr. Walker, smiling. "All scientists are gadget freaks—at least, most of them. I like them myself. I just can't afford them."

"But you've got friends who can," said Mr. Johnson, "and what are friends for?"

Their plans made, the men ate quickly and broke camp. The Johnsons had walked the trail to the north the evening before, so the group headed south. As agreed, Mr. Johnson poled the raft as Dr. Walker and Peter hiked the trail. Most of the time the two men on the trail could see the raft. When they could not, they periodically spoke over the radios.

At noon Mr. Johnson found a landing place, and the party reunited for lunch. They all agreed not to discuss the menu. While Mr. Johnson and Dr. Walker made plans for the afternoon, Peter followed a small stream to find a clear place from which to get water. He wore the radio for safety. When he had walked perhaps two hundred yards up the stream bed, he found the source of the stream—a small spring flowing from the mountainside and cascading down some six or seven feet. He reached out to fill his water bottles in the falls. While he was filling the last bottle, something yellow caught his eye. It had fallen quickly through the falls and was now floating downstream. He set his water bottles down and followed it. Within a few feet he had retrieved it. It was a yellow feather!

He hurried back upstream and pulled the brush away from the top of the falls. There above a small ledge was the mouth of a cave. He climbed up on the ledge for a better look. The cave opening was small, but it was big enough to enter. Still, he knew better than to go in alone. He put his hand over his eyes and peered into the darkness. When his eyes adjusted, he could see two shadowy figures. He moved a little further in to see them, then pressed the transmitter on his radio. "Dad, come quick!" he shouted. "Follow the stream bed up to the mountain. You gotta see this!"

Chapter 9
THE CAVE

Dr. Walker and Mr. Johnson came splashing up the middle of the stream bed, both breathing hard from the exertion.

"What is it, Peter?" called Mr. Johnson.

"I'd rather you see for yourself," he called from the ledge above the falls. Dr. Walker gave Mr. Johnson a boost up to the ledge. He, in turn, reached down and pulled up Dr. Walker. Both sat down to rest. "Give us a chance to catch our breath, and we'll be right with you," said Mr. Johnson. "We thought you were in trouble."

"I'm sorry, Dad. I guess I just got excited. But wait until you see what I found!"

Mr. Johnson looked at Dr. Walker, who nodded that he was ready. "Lead on, scout!" he said.

"Did you bring a flashlight?" Peter asked his dad.

"No. I didn't know we would need one."

Dr. Walker reached into his vest pocket and produced a small but extremely powerful flashlight. "Here, Peter. Use mine."

Peter grinned. "You should've been a secret agent. Look at this," he said, shining the small flashlight into the cave.

The small beam lit up the interior of the cave, revealing two statues, each about eight feet tall. The one on the left was a Gaboon viper, the same type snake that Mr. Johnson had killed on the trail. The statue on the right was a crocodile, its mouth open and threatening.

Dr. Walker took the light from Peter and walked to the snake for a closer inspection. He ran his hand along the creature's back. Then he found a place to stand at the rear of the statue and inspected its head. When he climbed down, he took a small camera from his pocket and snapped a picture. He then inspected the crocodile and took its picture.

"What do you make of it, Sam?" asked Mr. Johnson. "I've never seen this kind of work anywhere in Africa."

Dr. Walker shook his head. "I don't know, Steven. It's not contemporary African work, that's for sure. It's incredibly detailed and refined work and not styled like African statuary at all. I have seen some work in Egypt that was this highly detailed, but it didn't have the grace of these pieces."

He paused and smiled at his two friends. "Now, don't get me wrong. I'm not an art expert. But I think...well, I would say these show a definite Greek influence."

"Greek!" said a startled Peter.

"Mediterranean, anyway," replied Dr. Walker. "They don't look like modern work—say that of the Italian masters. They look ancient but refined. The Egyptians never did any work like this. And it isn't native to southern Africa. I can't even begin to offer you an explanation as to how they got here. But they look like fine Greek statues."

"Why are they here?" asked Peter.

"My guess is they're guarding the cave. They probably represent powerful spirits. They'd certainly keep most curiosity seekers out of here."

"But what about us? What are we going to do?" asked Mr. Johnson.

"We're going in," answered Dr. Walker. "But first we need to go back for our gear."

Mr. Johnson nodded. "We have pretty much everything we need. We've got about three hundred feet of rope. We've got food enough, if you'll pardon the expression, for perhaps two more days. The only thing that concerns me is light. I've got a flashlight, but it's only going to be good for a few more hours. And I think Peter's is about shot."

Peter nodded. "It wasn't too great when we got here; now it's pretty much dead."

"I've got two more of these in my pack," said Dr.

Walker, indicating the little flashlight in his hand. "They're all we need. The batteries are supposed to last a thousand hours."

"Great," said Mr. Johnson. "And I have four candles if we need them. We'd better bring everything with us. I don't want to leave any of our gear out there by the lake. It probably wouldn't be there when we got back."

The men returned to the campsite. They took everything out of their packs and laid it on the ground. After a careful inventory, they repacked it so they could easily find what they would need. Pulling the raft up on the bank as far as they could so that it would not float away, they headed back upstream to the cave.

As they entered, they stopped once more to look at its guardians, then they headed forward, single file, Dr. Walker taking the lead.

A small tunnel, not more than eight feet wide and about the same height, headed straight back into the mountain for about a hundred feet. Then it opened into a great cavern. The ceiling reached a height of perhaps seventy feet. Just inside the room the men found the spring that was the source of the stream they had been following. They were now without any kind of guide, and the cavern was filled with columns, stalactites and stalagmites, making it difficult to find a way across the floor. Mr. Johnson used duct tape to mark some of the columns so the party could find its way back to the spring.

After about two hundred feet, the floor suddenly smoothed out, and the ceiling lowered slightly. At this point in the cavern, the flashlights reached unobstructed to the walls on both sides. Dr. Walker moved toward the wall to his right. When about twenty feet from the wall, he stopped and worked the beam of his flashlight back and forth across the walls.

"What are you doing?" asked Peter.

"Just looking," answered Dr. Walker. "I wouldn't be surprised to find more artwork of some kind. When I was in France, I went to see the cave art at Lascaux. The best cave drawings were in an area just like this. I wondered if......there!"

Peter and Mr. Johnson looked at the spot where Dr. Walker's flashlight was focused. When they added their lights, they could make out dim drawings on the walls. Dr. Walker moved a little closer. "It's a dragon!" he exclaimed. "Look! It's a mural depicting a fight between the dragon and a group of hunters."

The excited scientist removed his pack and set it down. Quickly he found a small magnifying glass. He started to examine one of the figures on the mural. "I thought so, but now I'm sure of it. Steven, come look for yourself. These figures are

not dressed like African natives. They're dressed like Greeks!"

Mr. Johnson hurried over and took the magnifying glass. After a few moments, he looked at Dr. Walker and nodded his head. "I think you're right. But what—"

"Don't look at me," said Dr. Walker, shrugging his shoulders. "I'm as confused as you are."

"Are we talking about a lost culture or a colony?" asked Mr. Johnson.

"Could be. I just don't—"

"Dr. Walker! Look at this!" called Peter.

Dr. Walker stepped toward his young friend and looked at the place Peter was pointing his flashlight. "What is it?" he asked.

"Wings!" said Peter. "The thing has wings!"

Moving closer, Dr. Walker asked, "Are you sure?" shining his flashlight at the same spot.

"They're really dim," answered Peter, "but I'm sure that's what they are."

Dr. Walker inspected the dragon as closely as possible, but the figure was some twenty feet from the cave floor. "I wish I had a scaffold and some lights. I can't see well enough from here to be sure. But I believe you. I'm sure your eyes are better than mine."

"You mean you don't have a scaffold in your

equipment bag?" Peter asked, teasing.

"I considered bringing it, but then I remembered I'd have to carry it. Hey, Peter, look around a bit. Maybe we can find another dragon figure closer to the ground!"

After a thorough inspection of that part of the cavern, no other dragon figures were found. "Let's rest awhile; then we'll continue," said Dr. Walker. The others agreed, but after five minutes Peter walked back over to look at the winged dragon.

"Dr. Walker," he said, "do you really think the dragon could have had wings?"

"Why not? We do know there were winged dinosaurs. The pterodactyl, for instance, was really a lizard, but it flew."

Peter walked back and sat down. "Peter," said Mr. Johnson, "if that thing does have wings—and I'm not really sure it does—it would at least be consistent with the dragon legends. British folklore, as well as the Chinese accounts, spoke of winged dragons."

"That's right," agreed Dr. Walker. "The dragons were supposed to have flown great distances, attacking villages and farms at random. But there are no modern sightings of the winged dragons. All the sea monster and sea serpent sightings were snakelike animals or perhaps ocean-dwelling dinosaur types. Nobody claims to have seen a winged dragon in the past few hundred years."

Dr. Walker paused, then said, "Hey, this is interesting, but we'd better get moving again. Keep your eyes open for more paintings. Give me just a minute or so to photograph this mural, and we'll be on our way."

The room they had been exploring ended abruptly. A small passageway led from the room, turning to the left and declining rather steeply. At times the men had to hold onto the wall to keep from falling forward. After half an hour or so, the floor leveled out and the passageway widened.

This room was not high; neither was it rough. The floor, in fact, was smooth. The walls held no paintings. What was curious about the room was its odor. The men explored the room, beginning on the right and working their way around. Dr. Walker, who led the way, suddenly stopped at the edge of a deep hole. He shined his light into the dark pit. The walls of the pit were slick, and they curved downward under their feet.

Peter moved up to see, as did Mr. Johnson. "Where do you think that goes?" asked Peter.

"Don't know," answered Dr. Walker. "What do you think, Steven?"

"It might go back toward the lake. It smells like a sewer, so it might be wet down there," he answered.

"I'd sure like to see if that's true," said Dr.

Walker, "but there's no way we could get back out."

"I could go," said Peter. "Dad, we could make a harness like the ones we use when we climb. I could go down a ways just to see where it goes. Then you could pull me up."

Mr. Johnson shook his head. "No, it's too dangerous. If the rope broke, you'd just be stuck down there. You could never climb back up this way."

"But, Dad, we could use two ropes—or three! I would only go down a little way."

"No, Peter. Your mother would skin me alive if she found out I let you do that." Then he grinned. "She'd probably do it anyway if she knew we were in this cave."

Dr. Walker was still staring into the well. "I'll go," he said.

"What? But, Sam—"

"Nothing ventured, nothing gained. Just fix the harness and lower me down. My mother won't care."

Mr. Johnson chuckled. "You're a big boy. I just hope you know what you're doing."

"Hurry up before I change my mind."

Mr. Johnson and Peter rigged the harness, and Dr. Walker climbed in. Then the Johnsons lowered the scientist into the hole. He slid fifty feet or so along the bottom. Then he called out, "There's water down here! I can't go any farther. Pull me up!"

When Dr. Walker emerged from the hole, he looked shaken.

"Are you all right, Sam?" asked Mr. Johnson.

Dr. Walker answered weakly, "I'll be all right in a minute. That's a little hard on a fellow's nerves."

Peter grinned. "It's not easy going someplace like that, knowing you can't climb back out."

"That's only part of it," said Dr. Walker. "I was just sitting there on that damp floor getting my camera ready when I had a mental vision of the Leviathan coming out of that black water. I wanted out!"

Mr. Johnson helped Dr. Walker off with his harness and straightened out the ropes. At length, he asked, "Do you think that tunnel reaches the lake?"

"Probably," answered Dr. Walker. "Or there is an underground river. The tunnel may just drop right into the top of it. In either case, I'd say the tunnel is connected one way or another with the lake. I wish there was some way to find out."

"Could divers do it?"

Dr. Walker shook his head. "Way too dangerous. If there is a river, it could have currents. And there's no light. I wouldn't send anybody in there. And one thing's for sure—I ain't going!"

Peter laughed. "This is one time I'm with you. Even if you could go down there, you never know what you might run into. After seeing that painting

back there, I've got the 'willies.' I know we're probably not going to find that dragon, but if we do, I
want some place to RUN!"

Chapter 10
EVIDENCE

Dr. Walker picked up his pack and headed for the back of the cave. No one talked for a while as they followed another narrow passage farther back into the mountain. Dr. Walker longed for a change of clothes—he had been wearing these for four days. They had been sweated, soaked, smoked and, perhaps worst of all, he had spilled peach juice on them at breakfast. The night before, he had washed them, but they had dried slowly overnight and were stiff and mildewing. He was quite sure he was not alone in them, having picked up a few parasitic hitchhikers at some point. Now he had gotten them damp in the hole. He was in no mood for lighthearted conversation.

Apparently his friends' moods were no better. The ready wit and friendly jesting enjoyed during the first part of the trip had somewhat deteriorated. No one was really angry or sulking, but the edge had been taken off the trip by this difficult hike through the dark. And perhaps it was the dark that was most depressing of all. The small, bright flashlights made the trip possible and the footing easy to find, but they did little to dispel the surrounding gloom of the moist cave. So they walked quietly and steadily in single file toward the back of the cave.

Dr. Walker's thoughts headed home. He imagined Janet sitting by a cozy fire, comfortably reading and sipping her tea. She had come into his life at just the right time. The young professor had just taken his first full-time teaching assignment after spending several years on internship in the African plains. He had not really known that he was lonely—the work had fully absorbed him—but once he returned to the States and began teaching, he had realized just how alone he was.

He was on a busy campus, surrounded by energetic young students, but he had been a man alone. He was at least ten years older than most of his students, and he had little in common with them. Most of the professors were at least ten years older.

Then Janet had come. She was a graduate assistant with a master's degree in chemistry and a real love for animals. She had transferred in to work in the university's chemistry department as a lab assistant while pursuing her own doctorate. Janet was a ray of sunshine in an otherwise pretty stale chemistry department. In fact, she had made the whole science department fun. And Samuel Walker had been smitten at once. He had asked her to a birthday party for—

Suddenly Peter screamed.

Dr. Walker gasped and dropped his flashlight. He looked up where the other two flashlight beams were pointed. It was the dragon! Dr. Walker jumped backwards and nearly knocked Mr. Johnson down. "Hold it, Doc," said the steady voice of his friend. "It's just another statue. Peter, you okay?"

"Sure, Dad. I'm breathing. Now, if I can just get my heart to start beating again!"

Dr. Walker picked up his flashlight and focused its light on the huge gray dragon before him. The beam traveled up to its head, which had startled Peter. It was a magnificent piece of sculpture, with the same style and detail as the guardians. But it was much more fierce, much more sinister in its expression and aspect. Dr. Walker marveled as he worked his flashlight up and down the thirty-foot-high beast. If there had once been a monster such as this, he hoped it had been extinct for a long time.

"Dr. Walker, what's this hole in the body part for?" asked Peter. "It's so big you could climb in and sit down."

Dr. Walker looked inside the creature's body,

then answered, "I think it's an altar. There are ashes in here, and they don't look very old. What do you think, Steven?"

Mr. Johnson looked at the ashes, then pushed his hand in as far as he could. "They're still warm down here, Sam. I'd say it's been used sometime in the past four or five days."

Dr. Walker nodded. Then he worked the beam of his flashlight up the neck of the dragon once more. He looked at the ceiling above its head. "The smoke must come up through its mouth, eyes and nose. Then it must go up through those cracks in the ceiling."

"Uh huh," said Mr. Johnson. "Then when the smoke reaches the top of the mountain, it gets broken up by the trees. It would be real hard to spot during the day and all but impossible at night. Ingenious."

Dr. Walker pulled out his camera and took a whole roll of film of the dragon. He especially wanted a record of the magnificently sculpted head. "Let's sit down a minute," suggested Dr. Walker, when he had finished. "This is the end of the trip. The cave goes on from here, but this is as far as I go."

"Just as well," agreed Mr. Johnson, dropping his pack and settling down on the floor. "It's getting late, and we're going to have to start back in the morning. We're about out of food."

Peter walked around the room in which they found themselves. "That son of yours has the makings of a first-class scientist," said Dr. Walker. "You know he's got to be tired, but his curiosity keeps him on his feet."

"He's always been that way," admitted Mr. Johnson. "As much as I'd like for him to be a missionary, I think he's going to be happier doing something like you do."

"Well, the Lord needs scientists too. This world of ours is a skeptical place, and we need to help it understand that God's Word is the real source of truth. It gives us accurate information about our world. But the world is unwilling to accept it by faith. They need evidence—proof. Scientists with a Christian perspective on things can help with that. Some people are going to accept the Gospel only when they have been convinced on an intellectual level. Evidence that the Bible really is the Word of God helps them overcome the hurdle of their minds and reach out to the Gospel with their hearts."

"My dad was like that," said Mr. Johnson. "He had to know everything. He was a doctor and a natural skeptic. But he had Christian friends—also doctors—who convinced him that the Bible was not just a collection of Hebrew myths. Slowly he began to see it. When people prayed and his patients were healed, he couldn't just ignore that. And eventually he came to see that there was something to it. He began to read and study the Bible for himself. Finally he was convicted by what he read. He admitted that God was right and that he had been wrong. Then one of his friends was able to win him to Christ.

"Peter's like his grandfather. And I'm sure his grandfather has had some influence on him, but Peter had the advantage of putting his faith in Christ at an early age. He doesn't have to overcome years of training in skepticism. To him, the world is a great big adventure, and every mystery is an opportunity to discover for himself the truths that he believes already—just by faith. This Leviathan thing is not just poking around for evidence as far as he's concerned. He wants to find it to prove to the world that Job 41 is not just a fairy tale."

"So have we proven it?" asked Dr. Walker. "Take a look at that fellow up there behind me. Would you say that's the Leviathan?"

Mr. Johnson smiled. Just then Peter walked up. "I think it is," he said, firmly. "I just got in on the last question. What's up?"

"Just talking," said Dr. Walker, "but why do you say you think it is? I want to hear your opinion."

Peter settled down beside his father. "Well, just look at the description given in Job 41. Then check it off point by point with what we've discovered."

"Such as?"

"Well, let's start with his body. The Bible says that he's huge and strong, but that he's graceful. He's covered with scales. He has a rough underside. Did you notice the scales on the dragon behind you? And wouldn't you say he's strong and graceful?"

"Conceded," said Dr. Walker. "Go on."

"The Bible says he breathes fire. That altar behind you is designed to let the smoke and flames go up through his mouth and nose. Right?"

"Right. Go ahead."

"Well, let's see—oh, yeah—he has terrible teeth. And whoever carved that dragon made sure that part was obvious! Now, let's see. Um, that's all I can think of."

"That's pretty good," said Dr. Walker. "I can think of a couple more that we haven't come across yet. He lives in the water, and he leaves a wake of some kind."

"Could that be the slime?" asked Peter. "Maybe he uses it to get around somehow. That would leave a silvery trail—at least at night."

Dr. Walker shrugged his shoulders. "That could be one explanation for that passage about the wake. I just don't know. And speaking of slime, I haven't seen any in here. I had sort of hoped we would find out about that. But so far I haven't seen a trace of it."

"I'll look in the passage behind the altar," said Peter excitedly. "Maybe there's another room."

"You can look if you want to," said Mr. Johnson, "but if there's a room back there, don't go in. I'm tired, and I don't want to explore anymore. And if you go in there by yourself, you could get hurt."

"Yes sir," said Peter, and stood up. His knee popped, and he let out a little groan. "I guess I'm getting tired too. I think I'll look in the morning." With that, he opened his pack and unrolled his sleeping bag. "Wake me up for my watch." Within minutes the men could hear him breathing heavily.

"Are we going to post a watch tonight?" asked Dr. Walker.

"I think we'd better," said Mr. Johnson. "To tell you the truth, I wish we could get out of here tonight. I think we're going to have company tomorrow."

"What?"

"While you were talking about the Leviathan, I started thinking. See if you follow this. The natives who worship this Burong," he motioned with his hand toward the altar, "(assuming that's what we've got here) tried to keep us away. Then they wanted us to think nobody was here and that we were on a wild goose chase. But now that we've found their cave, which they were obviously hiding—"

"They won't let us go home to tell anybody!"

"Right. So I figure they'll be here sometime soon. They could kill us and just leave our bodies here in this cave. Brother Derrington and my wife would get people together to look for us, but they might never find the cave. We found it just because of a stray feather. They won't let that happen again."

Dr. Walker frowned. "I can just imagine being tossed in that hole back there. Steven, we need to pray together that God will protect us. And I think you're right. We need to sleep a few hours; then we need to get out of here!"

In the early hours of the morning Mr. Johnson shook Dr. Walker awake. Peter was already up and exploring. The pitch black of the cave was broken only by the flashlight beams of the two Johnsons. Dr. Walker felt around in his pack for his own light, then flicked it on. He hurt all over from sleeping on the stone floor, but he was ready for action. "I'll make breakfast if you haven't already done it," he said to his friend. "I know the menu—canned meat, canned peaches and crackers."

"Let me save you some trouble by simplifying the menu," replied Mr. Johnson. "We're out of crackers and canned peaches. All we have left is—"

"Don't say it," groaned Dr. Walker. "Let's just eat it and get out of here."

"Dad, Dr. Walker, I found something over here," called Peter. He was behind the altar, out of the sight of the two men. They walked over to see what he had discovered.

On the back side of the altar there was a small pile of what seemed to be equipment of some kind. The men focused their flashlights on the pile and began to sort it out. "This looks like a blowtorch of some kind," said Peter, holding up a small backpack with a nozzle.

"Peter, that's an old World War II flamethrower," said his father. "Put it down carefully. Now what do you suppose they'd want a flamethrower for? Do you think they use it in their rituals?"

"Maybe," said Dr. Walker, "but they may also have used it to burn down a couple of huts!"

"Possibility," said Mr. Johnson. "I wonder where they got it."

"Could have bought it anywhere in north Africa," answered the scientist. "The Allies left a lot of them in north Africa during the war. I've seen rangers use them on the Serengeti plains to clear brush from the roads. It's interesting that the natives would use it in their worship, though."

"I don't think it's all that unusual with these idol cults," said Mr. Johnson. "I've seen them use kerosene lanterns for burning incense, and I've heard of their figuring out uses for other kinds of war surplus and industrial equipment. They seem to be very adaptive."

"What's this?" asked Peter, holding up another item from the pile. "It looks like the bellows at the blacksmith shop back home in Pennsylvania."

"It is a bellows of some kind," agreed his dad. "Looks like the bellows part itself was worn out and they replaced it with an animal skin. Pretty neat job too. What do you think, Sam? Is this for the altar?"

"Probably. They might use it to fan the flames during their ceremonies. That would put sparks and flames up through the head of the dragon."

"Neat!" said Peter. "I'd like to see that!"

"Just use your imagination, Peter. We're not sticking around to see it demonstrated!"

"There's one more thing here," said Peter, handing the object to his dad. "Seems to be a trumpet made from some kind of horn. Dad, is this a cape buffalo horn?"

"Yes, Peter, it is. And look at this, Sam. It has a reed in it. It's not just a simple trumpet. It has a vibrating reed!"

Dr. Walker took it from Mr. Johnson. "I'll bet it sounds great! You know, I'll bet that's the scream the natives at Marjao heard during the attack.

You know, fellows, with all this stuff, those natives could have pulled off the entire Burong attack themselves."

"But what about the footprints?" asked Peter.

"If we knew where to look, I think we'd probably find something for making footprints. You remember those prints didn't seem deep enough to have been made by a big animal. I think they staged the whole thing."

"Well, it was pretty convincing," said Peter. "And that horn probably scared everybody so bad they couldn't think straight."

"You're probably right," replied Dr. Walker. "It must make an awful racket."

"Try it out, Dr. Walker," said Peter.

"Not in here. It would probably break our eardrums."

"Besides," said Mr. Johnson, with a chuckle, "you might blow a mating call by mistake!"

The three of them had a good laugh, then packed quickly, took pictures of the newly discovered items and got on their way.

The walk back didn't take long, because they weren't exploring. They followed their markers and took the shortest path across the big chambers. When they went by the deep hole, they automatically picked up the pace. Dr. Walker could feel the hair rising on the back of his neck.

Soon they were standing just inside the mouth of the cave. Mr. Johnson moved up carefully, cautiously staying in the shadows, aware that someone could be watching. After remaining motionless for several minutes, moving only his head to scan the jungle on either side, he crept back into the cave.

"There doesn't seem to be anybody out there," he said, "but we can't be sure. Let's go on, but keep your eyes open, and be as quiet as we can."

The three worked their way down the stream bed toward the lake. When they were within thirty feet of the raft, they suddenly heard movement in the jungle behind them.

"Run for the raft!" shouted Mr. Johnson, and the three of them made a quick dash for their only means of escape. When they reached the raft, they used their combined strength to launch it. Loud shrieks came from the jungle behind them. The three men expected any moment to feel a spear or a dart pierce their backs. But none came. As Dr. Walker and Mr. Johnson rowed with all their might, Peter looked back toward the shore. He saw about forty men, their bodies painted green, moving from the jungle. He shouted to his father and to Dr. Walker. They turned to look.

"Dad, why did they stop chasing us?"

"I don't know, Peter. Maybe they figured we

were heading to the south shore. They can beat us there on the trail, you know. Just for that reason, I think we'd better head for that nearest island."

"I think I know another reason," added Dr. Walker. "Look where those natives stopped. They must be fifty feet from the shore. I think they're scared to death to get close to the water!"

Chapter 11
THE ISLAND

The men rowed their raft toward the island while Peter steered. They watched the green-painted natives work their way along the trail to the south end of the lake. Before the raft had reached the island, the natives had reached the south shore, cutting off the path of escape.

Because they had left the cave in the early morning, they were able to row the five or so miles to the island by midmorning. Exhausted, they pulled the raft halfway onto the bank and collapsed. There they dozed until noon.

Dr. Walker woke up first, his mouth dry and his temples pounding. He had found a spot to lie down without too much thought of cover, and he had been lying in the hot sun for almost two hours. He turned over and got to his hands and knees, reaching for his canteen. To his dismay, it was almost empty. He drank sparingly, then shook Mr. Johnson awake.

"What is it?" asked Mr. Johnson, sitting up and

staring at Dr. Walker with wide, groggy eyes. "Something wrong?"

"I'm afraid so. Did you fill your canteen before we left the cave?"

A look of horror passed over Mr. Johnson's face. He reached for his canteen. It was about halfway full. "I can't believe it! How could I be so stupid?"

"You mean *we,* don't you? Mine's got less in it than yours. How about Peter's?"

Mr. Johnson walked over to where his son lay, opened Peter's pack and picked up his canteen. It was almost empty. Peter woke up when he heard his dad fumbling with his pack. "Everything okay, Dad?"

"Not too good, Peter. We're about out of water."

"Oh no!" groaned Peter, sitting up wearily. "How could we forget to fill our canteens?"

"Don't beat yourself up over it. I'm the one who should take the blame. I was in such a hurry to get away from that cave that I completely overlooked it. Didn't you have an extra water bottle in your pack?"

"Yeah, that's right!" said Peter. He reached into the bottom of his pack and found the quart water bottle. "It's not big, but it'll help."

"Steven," said Dr. Walker, "we're going to need help. We can't get off this island, and I'm pretty sure we won't find any water here. And we have hardly any food. We need to pray that God will help us."

"You're right, Sam. Let's do that now."

The three men bowed their heads right on the spot. Dr. Walker voiced their prayer: "Dear Lord, we know that we are in Your hands. You see us even in this jungle. We ask that You take care of us in this situation. We want to be able to get back to the mission station safely. We believe that You have more work for us to do. We also ask that You would supply us with food and water. Lord, we ask that You send Clyde Derrington here with help. And, Lord, we ask that You help us reach these people there on the shore with the Gospel of the Lord Jesus Christ. It is probable that none of them has ever heard the Gospel. We would like to see them saved, and we know that would please You also. Thank You in advance for Your deliverance. In Christ's name we pray. Amen."

When Dr. Walker finished his prayer, the men set out to do what they could to set up camp. While the Johnsons set up the tents and collected firewood, Dr. Walker took a walk around the island to see if he could find a spring. The island was small and covered with undergrowth. The vegetation was not as thick as that on the south shore, but nonetheless travel was difficult. He hacked his way through with Mr. Johnson's machete. Within two hours he had completely circled the island, unsuccessful at finding any source of water. But he had time to think, and by the time he reached camp he had come up with two things to try.

The Johnsons had by this time set up camp and were resting under the shade of the trees. As the sun lowered, it passed on the northern side of the island. The canopy formed by the trees provided shelter from the lowering sun, and the slight breeze coming off the water made the afternoon bearable. Dr. Walker arrived back at camp hot and tired.

"Sit down, Sam," said Mr. Johnson, "before you fall down. What did you find?"

"Nothing. Just an island. I really didn't expect to find a spring, but I thought I'd look anyway. But I did come up with some ideas."

"Really? What?"

"Well, as you know, many of these plants and trees soak up water like sponges. That way they can survive during the dry season. We might be able to cut them open and get the water out."

"You mean like you cut open a cactus?" asked Peter.

"Exactly. And even if it doesn't taste good, the moisture will keep us alive until help gets here. And I thought of something else. I've had all my equipment, except for the night scope, which was in a waterproof case, wrapped in ordinary, plastic food wrap. We could set up a water trap using that plastic water bottle of Peter's. If it rains, we could funnel the water into the bottle. And if it rains enough, we might be able to fill all the canteens as well."

"That's a good idea—*if* it rains," said Mr. Johnson. "Let's get it built just in case we get a late afternoon shower. We haven't had one in the six days since we left the mission station, but that's no reason it can't happen. It's awfully hot today, and the heat might cause a thunderstorm when it starts to get dark. It's sure worth a try."

Following Dr. Walker's instructions, Mr. Johnson cut down two small trees and stripped off the branches from them. Then he connected the two trees by the narrow tops. He then lashed a brace onto the two trees to form a triangle. In the meantime, Dr. Walker unwrapped several pieces of equipment and carefully laid the plastic wrap on the ground. When Mr. Johnson had finished the frame, they laid the plastic wrap across it in layers. The whole thing was then tied between two trees with the pointed end on the ground, in a V shape. The end of the V was then placed in the mouth of the water bottle, which was braced with several rocks to prevent it from falling over.

"That's neat," said Peter, inspecting the finished trap. "Now if it will just rain!"

By midafternoon clouds were building up. They had prayed for at least a brief shower, but when late afternoon arrived without a shower, Dr. Walker began to feel that perhaps the whole project had been a waste of time.

"I'm going to start looking for some water-bearing plants," he told his friends. "I won't be gone long. What's our food situation?"

"Not good," answered Mr. Johnson. "We have just one can of meat left."

"I hate that stuff," said Peter, "but I'll miss it when it's gone."

"Did you find anything edible when you went on your walk?" asked Mr. Johnson.

"Nothing I could recognize," answered Dr. Walker. "There may be hundreds of edible plants here on the island, but I don't know what they are. And there aren't many animals. I saw a few mice, but I'm not that hungry."

"Yet!" added Mr. Johnson. "I have an idea. I have some fishing line and hooks in my survival kit. Why don't I use the rest of the canned meat as bait?"

"That might work," commented Dr. Walker. "It's certainly worth a try."

"I don't know, Dad," said Peter. "I don't think fish would eat it. They're too smart for that."

Dr. Walker chuckled. "Well, maybe these fish can be fooled into thinking it's food. At any rate, go ahead and try. I will be back in just a few minutes." With that, he started into the rough jungle undergrowth.

When he returned, he was carrying several different kinds of plants. "How's the fishing?" he called to his friends. Peter held up a forked stick with several small fish on it. "We've caught a few little ones, but nothing that looks very good. Did you find any vegetables?"

"A few of these look promising, but I don't know whether to eat them or squeeze them."

Peter smiled. "You want me to help?"

"No, just keep at it. I really don't know what I'm doing, so I don't know how you could help."

"Sam, come over here a minute," Mr. Johnson called to Dr. Walker from a makeshift table by the raft. "I've been trying to clean one of these little fish. They're all bones! I don't think we could make one meal if we caught fifty. Any suggestions?"

Dr. Walker said, "When I went fishing with my dad and we had a bad day, Dad used to cut up a small fish as bait. He would throw it out farther and deeper than we had been fishing. Sometimes a big fish would be following the little ones, and he would hit it. Worked more than once."

"I'll try it!" said Mr. Johnson, and he put the head of one of the little fish on the hook. "I think I'll need a weight of some kind. Maybe I can find a stone that will work."

"Hold on a minute, Steven." Dr. Walker walked to his pack and took out the lightweight tripod for his camera. Then he took a large wing nut off the tripod. "Here—try this."

Mr. Johnson tied the wing nut on the line, walked out to the raft, and threw the line out into the lake as far as he could. He then took the hand-line and tied it to a stout stick. "Better be ready just in case," he said.

Peter caught several more of the tiny fish, then came to the raft. "I'm out of bait," he said. "That's the last of the canned meat. I've got fifteen of these little ones. I just don't think they're going to make much of a meal. What did you put on that line out there?"

When his dad told him what they were trying, Peter was anxious to try it as well. Soon he had rigged his line like his father's. He walked back down the shore where he had been fishing and threw in his line.

Dr. Walker beat on his plants and squeezed and ground and tested, but he came up with nothing. "Why didn't I study botany instead of zoology?" he said at last to no one in particular. "If we ate this muck, I'm sure we'd all fold up and die screaming."

"Couldn't be any worse than that other muck we've been eating," said Peter, walking up behind him.

Dr. Walker laughed and assured, "Yes, it could, though it might not taste any worse!"

"How you doin' down there, Dad?" called Peter. "We need you to catch our main course for us. Dr. Walker has struck out with the soup and salad."

"Nothing yet," called Mr. Johnson. "We may have to go without supper tonight. Hey, Peter, why don't you go over there and ask those green fellows what they eat?" he continued, indicating the natives on the south shore. "They're lighting fires all up and down the bank. Look's like they're getting ready for a feast. Maybe they'll share something with us."

"Sure, Dad. I'll go right over. I'm sure they'd like to have *us* for dinner."

"Poor choice of words," said Dr. Walker, smiling grimly.

Suddenly Mr. Johnson gave a yelp. The stick he had been holding nearly came out of his hand. He stood and began to struggle with the fish he had hooked. "Hey, come help me!" he yelled. "I've hooked a monster!"

Man, I hope he's wrong, thought Dr. Walker. "Coming!" he yelled.

He and Peter ran to the raft. Peter tied a rope to his dad's belt and ran to tie it to a tree. "Don't lose him, Dad. I'm hooking you up so we don't lose you!" Then Peter ran back to the raft. Dr. Walker stood there helpless, watching the big man fight the fish.

Mr. Johnson had no reel, so he could not fight the fish as a sport fisherman might do—letting the fish run until it was tired. He was just wrestling with it for possession of the line. "Don't break the line, Steven," offered Dr. Walker. "Ease up when you can."

"He shouldn't be able to break this line," said Mr. Johnson between gasps. "It's eighty-pound test. If he does break something, it'll probably be my arm!"

Mr. Johnson fought valiantly for about fifteen minutes. Every time the fish came toward the raft, he wound the line around his stick. When the fish swam away from the raft, they could only pray the line didn't break. Suddenly the fish turned toward the raft in a rush across the top of the water. Mr. Johnson turned and leaped from the raft and onto the shore and continued running up the bank and into the woods. The fish hit the raft and was stunned. Peter grabbed the line and pulled the fish around the raft and started to pull it up on shore.

"Wait, Peter!" yelled his father. "Look out for its teeth!"

"Teeth!" shouted Peter, instantly letting go of the line. The fish surged away, but Mr. Johnson had been reeling in the line, and the fish was tiring. It came back toward shore as Mr. Johnson pulled its head around.

"Sam, grab something to hit it with. I'm going to try to work it up on the raft. Peter, get my leather gloves!"

Peter took off for the tent, and Dr. Walker began searching for a stick. Finally he found a sturdy one that would work.

Peter ran back with his father's gloves. Mr. Johnson held out one hand, and Peter put the glove on his father's hand. "That'll have to do," said the older man. "Now, Sam, get ready." Mr. Johnson grabbed the line, wrapped it around his hand once and pulled. The big fish eased out of the water and onto the raft. Dr. Walker raised the club to strike. Just then, the fish thrashed its tail in one last desperate attempt to escape. Dr. Walker hit the fish a glancing blow and fell forward. The fish made a lightning-quick movement and ripped open the young scientist's leg. Dr. Walker hit the fish again.

"Look out!" yelled Peter. He grabbed Dr. Walker by the shirt and yanked backwards. Dr. Walker fell on the raft, and Peter shot the fish once in the head. It lay still, dead where it was shot.

"Well done, Peter," said Dr. Walker. Then he reached for his pant leg. It was soaked with blood.

Mr. Johnson dragged the heavy fish on shore to his makeshift table, then went to see about Dr. Walker's wound. "How is it, Sam?"

Dr. Walker was rolling up his pant leg. "I don't think I'll die from it, but it hurts something awful!"

Mr. Johnson examined the wound. "I'm not sure I agree with you, Sam. If we don't get this thing disinfected, you could die from it. At least it's not bleeding too much. Let me get my emergency first aid kit and clean it up. But I'm afraid it's going to take the rest of our good water."

"Oh, no," said Dr. Walker. "I'm sorry."

"That's okay. The Lord knows about it. He'll provide for us." Mr. Johnson ran to his tent and returned with the first aid kit. He used an alcohol prep to clean the wound. Dr. Walker held his breath and nearly passed out from pain.

"That's nasty," said Mr. Johnson. "Some of these cuts are half an inch deep. I had no idea that fish had such long teeth. Peter, open two—no, three—of those sterile gauze pads. We'll put them on the cuts in just a second. Ready, Doc?"

Dr. Walker nodded. He was sure the ground was moving under him.

Mr. Johnson told Peter to place the pads on the cuts, overlapping the edges. He opened a long bandage roll and began to wrap the leg. Dr. Walker groaned. Mr. Johnson stopped to put a roll of gauze in the doctor's mouth. Dr. Walker bit down on the gauze while Mr. Johnson finished wrapping the leg. When the job was finished, Dr. Walker lay down on his back. The ground continued to spin as it turned from green to orange and back.

Mr. Johnson cleaned the fish and began to fry long strips of the lighter colored meat. Dr. Walker stirred and raised himself on his elbows. "That smells good," he said weakly.

"No, it doesn't," said Mr. Johnson, smiling. "It just smells different from that canned stuff. How's the leg?"

"It feels terrible." Just then, a drop of water landed on his shirt. Then another hit him on the arm. He looked overhead and saw that it was beginning to rain.

Chapter 12
ATTACK!

The fish tasted better than Dr. Walker had expected. He didn't know for sure whether it really tasted all that good or whether it was just the change in diet that seemed so welcome. In any case, he grinned to himself when he thought of that dinner in terms of "revenge." And the rain had filled all the water bottles. Both their prayers concerning food and water had been answered, for which they thanked God.

After dinner, Dr. Walker hobbled back to his tent and lay on his sleeping bag. His leg hurt and his mind seemed clouded. His head ached as well. Thoughts of home raced through his mind, and every few minutes he thought about the possibility of being rescued. *This is the sixth day since we left the mission station,* he said to himself. *On the third day, we reached the lake. Then on the fourth, we explored the east side of the lake and crossed. On the fifth, we explored the west side and found the cave. On the sixth—was that this morning?*

Seems like a week ago—we came to the island. Okay. Now, if the bearers who left us headed straight back to the village, which is likely, they would have gotten back—when? Probably the afternoon of the fourth day. Let's see. If Clyde organized a party to come get us, then he would have left the next morning or perhaps the same day. Then he would be here—today! Or tomorrow, at the latest.

"Dr. Walker?" It was Peter.

"Come in."

"Were you talking—"

"Just thinking out loud, Peter. I can't think too clearly, so I was trying to work something out in my head—when we are going to get rescued."

"Dad says he thinks Rev. Derrington will be here tomorrow."

Dr. Walker nodded. "I think so too. Sometime in the early afternoon—maybe even late morning. They'll probably travel faster than we did."

"Dad said you might want these." Peter handed Dr. Walker two white pills.

"What are they?"

"Pain pills of some kind."

Dr. Walker took the pills and swallowed them down with water from his canteen. "Thanks, Peter," he said, lying back down. "You're a saint.

Your dad too. My head was splitting. I think I'd better go to sleep now."

"Dad said not to worry about your watch, Dr. Walker. We'll get by all right."

But Dr. Walker did not hear. He was already asleep.

Sometime in the middle of the night Dr. Walker awoke. All was completely quiet. Too quiet. Earlier the natives on the opposite shore had been milling around their fires. They were building them up high, constantly collecting firewood for the fires. But now there was no noise from the south shore.

The Johnsons and Dr. Walker had discussed the natives' fire-building activities at dinner. Why were they building such big fires? To keep away wild animals? Or something else?

But now there was no activity from them at all. Dr. Walker got painfully to his feet and hobbled out of the tent. Peter sat by the fire, which had burned down to just a few coals. The night was dark, the clouds overhead obscuring the moon and stars. So Dr. Walker took his little flashlight from his pocket and flipped it on. Peter turned and looked back. "Dr. Walker, is that you?"

"Yes. Everything all right?"

"I don't know," answered Peter. "The natives seem to have left. At least, I can't hear anybody over there."

"Maybe they're just sleeping."

"I don't think so. I could hear them talking about an hour ago. They seemed nervous or something. They started moving around, and then everything got quiet. I could see them by the light of their fires. Then they just weren't there anymore. It's so dark out here I can't see a thing."

"Why don't you get my night scope from my tent?" suggested Dr. Walker. "We'll see what's going on over there."

Peter wasted no time complying. He had wanted to do that very thing, but he hadn't wanted to disturb Dr. Walker. He hurried back with the scope and set it up near the shore.

In a few seconds, he had it turned on and focused. "They're gone," he said at length. "No sign of them anywhere." He worked the scope back and forth, scanning the shoreline. Suddenly, something in the water near the far shore caught his attention. He saw it for a moment; then it was gone.

"Dr. Walker, I just saw something in the water," he said, turning away from the scope for just a moment. "Then it disappeared."

"Probably a crocodile."

Peter shook his head. "Crocodiles always swim with their bodies under water," he said. "This looked more like a hippo. It was high out of the water."

"See if you can find it again. I'd come look, but I

think I'd better just sit here. My leg is killing me."

Peter scanned the lake for some time. He saw nothing but the small waves of the lake stirred by the night breeze. But wait! There in the middle of the lake. What was that? Bubbles? Rings in the water?

"Dr. Walker, I know it's hard for you, but could you come and look at this?"

Dr. Walker pulled himself against the trunk of a tree and walked over to the scope. He sat down and leaned over to see through the scope. He watched for a few seconds, then looked at Peter. "What did you see?"

"It looked like bubbles. And movement under the water—you know, rings like when you throw a stone in the water."

Dr. Walker looked once more. Then he began to move the scope back and forth. Suddenly, he saw it too. He looked up from the scope toward the lake. There it was. Now he couldn't make out the bubbles, but there was a faint glow from the surface of the water. "Peter, look!" he whispered excitedly. "Do you see the glow on the water?"

"Yes," answered Peter. "What could it be? I'm going to get Dad." With that, he scurried off toward his tent.

When the Johnsons returned, Dr. Walker was looking through the scope. Something was out there. But what? Dr. Walker continued to follow the ring of waves with the scope. Every now and then he could see the glowing.

"There. Did you see it, Dad?"

"Yes. Sam, what do you think it is?"

"I don't know. But whatever it is, the natives saw it first—and they lost no time leaving. I think we ought to figure out what we're going to do if it comes this way."

"I've got my guns and two boxes of shells," said Mr. Johnson. "I'll get them. Do you know how to fire a pistol?"

"I can use your revolver," said Dr. Walker.

"Okay. I'll be right back."

Dr. Walker looked back through the scope, but he could not see the bubbles or the glow. Where had it gone? Could he have imagined it? No, the Johnsons had seen it too.

Peter was straining to see into the blackness. He edged closer to shore.

Suddenly the water boiled up. There was movement in the water, splashing near the raft. Dr. Walker reached into his pocket for his flashlight and turned it on. There, some twelve or fifteen feet above the water, was the head of the dragon. Its eyes glowed yellow, and smoke billowed from its nostrils. He screamed at Peter to run back, but Peter's feet were frozen to the ground.

Dr. Walker turned off the flashlight and started backing up. "Peter, get out of there! Move!" His continued cries finally got through to Peter, so he started backing away. The dragon shrieked. It raised itself further from the water and unfolded its wings. Peter turned to run toward Dr. Walker. "Dad!" he screamed. "Help!"

Mr. Johnson was suddenly standing beside Dr. Walker. He handed the scientist the pistol and a box of shells. "Here," he said, quietly. "It's loaded."

"Peter!" he called in a firm but calm voice. "Be quiet. Walk. That's right, just keep coming. Maybe if we stay calm, it will just move back into the water. Good boy. Here," he said, tossing a flare gun to Peter. "If it attacks, shoot it at him. Maybe it'll frighten him away."

The dragon stayed where it was. He seemed to be studying the men before him. It sniffed the air. Then it attacked.

Its first movements were a half jump, half step onto the raft, which flew to pieces under the dragon's crushing weight. The creature rushed toward the men.

"Now!" cried Mr. Johnson, opening fire. Peter fired the white phosphor flare into the dragon's face. It screamed in pain and fright, and it shook its head from side to side. Dr. Walker and Mr. Johnson emptied their guns into the beast. It shrieked in pain and backed away. Mr. Johnson ran out of shells and stopped to reload. Dr. Walker fired twice more, then did the same.

In that brief instant, the dragon rushed at them headlong. Mr. Johnson started firing again, while Dr. Walker fumbled with his pistol. The dragon covered the short distance with incredible speed.

Mr. Johnson stood firm and fired at the dragon's head. "Go for the eyes!" he called. "It's our only chance!" Dr. Walker stood up and fired. One of the dragon's eyes went out. The beast screamed in agony and backed away. It seemed to be tiring of the battle.

Then it stretched out its neck and let loose a fiery blast. The flames shot through the air and hit Dr. Walker full force. He screamed and fell to the ground, on fire from the waist down. Mr. Johnson ran to him and began to roll him on the ground to put out the flames. He beat on his clothing until the flames were extinguished.

Peter had grabbed a shovel. He took a shovel full of coals and threw them into the creature's face, screaming like a madman.

The creature shrieked again, then opened his enormous mouth and grabbed Peter by the head and shoulders. It jerked the boy from the ground like a rag doll, his arms and legs flailing. Then the dragon turned and lumbered off toward the water.

Mr. Johnson gave chase, firing into the dragon from close range. It swung its great tail and slammed it into Mr. Johnson. Dr. Walker watched in horror as Mr. Johnson struck the ground and lay there motionless. The dragon continued into the water and disappeared from sight, carrying his dinner with him.

Dr. Walker lay there on the ground in total agony of mind and body. In a few seconds the water returned to its inky calm. The night was again quiet. Mr. Johnson did not move.

And Peter was gone.

Chapter 13
REALITY

The light streaming in through the tent door awakened Dr. Walker. He started to roll over, but the pain in his leg jerked him to wide-awake consciousness. He sat up and reached toward his wound. He looked down to see what damage had been done the night before—but wait a minute! His leg was hurting, but his pants were not burned! His pant leg was neatly stitched with a piece of fishing line. What...?

"Dr. Walker?" called a voice from outside the tent. "Are you all right?" It was Peter!

"Peter! Come in!" When the boy came in, Dr. Walker pulled him to him and hugged him tightly.

"Dr. Walker, are you all right?" repeated Peter when he could catch his breath.

"Just great! My leg hurts, but I'm fine! And you're fine! And your dad?"

"He's fine too," answered the bewildered boy. "Let me go get him."

"Yes! Go get him!" cried the jubilant man.

Peter was worried about his friend, so he hurried to get his dad. When they returned, Dr. Walker was still smiling from ear to ear. Mr. Johnson put his hand on the doctor's forehead.

"Good. The fever broke. I was worried about you last night."

"I was worried about you too!"

"Me? Why were you worried about me?"

"Let me explain it later," said Dr. Walker, "when we're out of here! How are things?"

"No sign of Clyde or the villagers. No water or food. But otherwise we're all right. I guess things could be worse."

"Much worse," agreed Dr. Walker. "Take my word for it."

Peter shook his head. "I wish I knew what you were talking about. You were so sick last night you passed out. You started groaning in the middle of the night. Your temperature went way up, and I think you were delirious for a while. You kept screaming and calling—well, calling my name. It was kind of scary."

"I hope I didn't keep you up all night," said the scientist, smiling. "I feel much better now. But my leg still feels like it's going to come off."

Mr. Johnson had raised Dr. Walker's pant leg

and was looking at the bandages. "I hope we can avoid that," he said. "But we're going to have to get you off this island and back to the mission station. It's almost noon. I wish Derrington would get here."

"He'll come," said Dr. Walker, earnestly. "You know he will."

"Yes, I know. And we can survive here for a while, I'm sure. But you need to get back to the infirmary. I'm going to change that bandage now, and you're not going to like it."

"Go ahead. It's not as bad as it could be. Just give me something to bite down on."

Changing the bandage was an ordeal. Dr. Walker winced and groaned, but he didn't cry out. In a few minutes, he was lying back down on his sleeping bag. Beads of perspiration stood out on his forehead, and his shirt was soaked. But his leg actually felt better. When he was a little stronger, Mr. Johnson gave him some more pain pills.

"The natives are still on the south shore," Mr. Johnson said. "I'm sure they have lookouts posted. We'll know when Derrington's party gets here. There will be a commotion over there. I just hope he brings enough villagers with him. I'd hate for Brother Clyde to be attacked."

"Help me outside," said Dr. Walker. "It's awfully hot in here. And I want to see what's going on."

Mr. Johnson helped the scientist outside and

placed him against a tree where he could watch the shore. Dr. Walker made himself as comfortable as possible and prayed that Rev. Derrington and the natives would come soon.

The natives on the south shore were just sitting by their dying fires. Dr. Walker knew they were watching him and the Johnsons. *What were they thinking? What were their plans?*

Suddenly there was a piercing shriek. Dr. Walker jumped involuntarily. He looked toward the water. Was there...?

Then the natives on the south shore jumped to their feet and started running down the trail toward the cave. The blast was repeated again and again. Mr. Johnson and Peter ran to Dr. Walker. "That must be that cape buffalo trumpet!" shouted Peter.

Mr. Johnson agreed. "That's probably a signal of some kind. Maybe they've seen Clyde's group!"

"I hope you're right," said Dr. Walker, his heart still pounding in his chest. That was the same shriek he had heard in his wild dreams. He could not help but look up and down the length of the lake. He half expected to see the Leviathan stirring itself and rising to attack.

Peter grabbed his binoculars and ran to the raft. He looked toward the trail from Marjao. After a few minutes he let out a whoop.

"There they are! Brother Derrington is leading the way. And he has the chief with him. And there must be a hundred men with them!"

Peter jumped lightly from the raft and ran to the tent. "Let's get this stuff packed and go home!"

Dr. Walker sat on the raft and waved to his friends on the south shore while the Johnsons packed his things. Peter came walking back, pale and quiet.

"What's wrong, Son?" asked Mr. Johnson, who had just finished packing his and Dr. Walker's things on the raft.

"Dad, I found something while I was putting everything in my pack. I must have accidentally brought it from the cave."

"What is it?"

"This," and he handed his father the cape buffalo trumpet.

Dr. Walker and Mr. Johnson stared at the black object. "Well," said Mr. Johnson at last, "cape buffalo do have *two* horns!"

"Right," said Dr. Walker. "Sure. Uh huh. Say, Steven..."

"Yes?"

"Let's get out of here!"

Within an hour the three friends were reunited with Rev. Derrington. The raft crossing had been uneventful but also uncomfortable for Dr. Walker. He was glad when he was sitting on a campstool, eating *real* food. Rev. Derrington was full of questions, and Dr. Walker and the Johnsons filled him in on the events of the past seven days.

Finally, Dr. Walker was worn out. "I'm sorry, Clyde. I'm going to have to rest. Maybe Steven and Peter can finish this story for you."

"You just take it easy," said Rev. Derrington. "I'll get my answers in time. It sounds like you've had quite a week! We can talk later."

Dr. Walker slept through the afternoon and night. In the morning he was ready to travel. The party was put in order, and they were ready to move. Just as they were starting on the trail, the four bearers who had disappeared came to see Dr. Walker. They had the missionary with them. "Sam, these men wanted me to convey their apologies to you."

"Tell them I'm glad to see them and that I'm glad they are all right. By the way, Clyde, what happened to them?"

"They were attacked in the middle of the night by those green-painted fellows," he explained. "They were tied up and carried off. Then they were tied to trees. This fellow here," he said, placing his hand on a broad-shouldered giant, "is Bolgi. He's as strong as an ox, and he managed to break the vines they had used to tie him. Then he freed the others. They tried to figure out whether to follow you or to come back and get help. They finally decided they had better get back. They traveled all day and all night to reach the village."

"Tell them I thank them for bringing help," said Dr. Walker. He smiled at the four men. "Thank you."

The men smiled and looked pleased. They nodded their heads and reached out to shake Dr. Walker's hand. He smiled and shook their hands in turn. "Thank you, friends."

"By the way, Sam," said Rev. Derrington, "these men have volunteered to carry you back. Steven helped them build a litter."

Dr. Walker smiled again and nodded at the men. "Thank you, friends."

"Walker friend," said Bolgi.

As they traveled through the jungle, the villagers began chattering excitedly. One of them was holding something. He brought it to Rev. Derrington, who carried it to Dr. Walker.

"The natives found this snakeskin pinned to a tree," he said. "Do you know anything about this?"

"Yes," said Dr. Walker, taking the skin from the missionary. "The snake attacked us on the trail—actually, I think those green-skinned fellows meant it as a 'go-away present.' Steven shot it and skinned it out for me as a souvenir. I'm glad we found it. I had forgotten all about it."

"These skins are highly valued among the villagers," said Rev. Derrington. "It takes great courage to kill a Gaboon viper. It's extremely valuable. That's why the natives were so excited."

"Call the chief," said Dr. Walker. "I want to speak to him."

Rev. Derrington called to some villagers standing nearby. Soon all the villagers were gathered around Dr. Walker, the missionaries and their chief.

"Please translate for me, Clyde," said Dr. Walker. Rev. Derrington nodded. "My friend the chief risked his life and all his people to save Mr. Johnson, Peter and myself," he began. "He is worthy of thanks and honor. I want to show my friendship and gratitude. Here is the skin of a great viper that attacked me on the way to Nyvasu Mweri. My friend Steven Johnson killed it. Now I want to give it to you, Chief, as a token of my gratitude. Thank you for being my friend."

The chief took the skin and held it up for all the villagers to see. They murmured their approval. The chief ran his hand over the scales. He turned back to Dr. Walker. "You are great friend," he said in his own tongue. "Walker is my friend. He is good man like Derrington." Then he came to the young scientist and hugged him. The natives chuckled and clapped.

The chief came to the fire that night to talk to Rev. Derrington and Dr. Walker. He had many questions. First, why had the missionary risked his own life by returning to the mission station when he had been threatened? Why had Dr. Walker come with the missionary? Didn't he know the danger he faced? Why would Dr. Walker and the Johnsons risk their lives by traveling to Nyvasu Mweri? Did they not know the dangers they would face? His questions were sincere. He was genuinely bewildered by their actions. He could not understand why white men would face such dangers willingly.

Rev. Derrington glanced at Dr. Walker, then began to answer the old chief. "We were willing to face these dangers because we love you and your people." The old chief started to interrupt, but Rev. Derrington held up his hand. "Please let me explain. You have been to our meetings. You have heard the story of Jesus Christ."

The old chief nodded.

"Jesus lived in Heaven with His Father," the missionary continued. "He did not have to come to earth to live among men. But Jesus and His Father knew that unless Jesus came to earth and died for men, all men would perish and spend eternity in Hell because of their sins. Eternity is a long time that never ends. And Jesus and His Father loved men. The Bible, God's Word, tells us that God was not willing to let men die. So Jesus came to earth knowing that He would die for men. And God accepted His sacrifice for sin and raised Him from the dead.

"Now Jesus lives to save those who will come to Him. Because Jesus died and was raised from the dead, we can all be saved from this eternal Hell. Jesus will forgive us of our sins if we but ask Him.

"We belong to Jesus," he said, indicating himself and Dr. Walker. "We must do what He commands. And He has told us in the Bible to tell this story, the story of man's deliverance from sin, to all the people of the world. We came to tell you this story. And because God loved us, He has made us to love you too. We will do whatever is necessary to bring you the story of God's love. And we will do whatever is necessary to help you understand and believe it."

The chief looked at Rev. Derrington through tear-filled eyes. He was obviously moved. "You have given your lives just like your Jesus did. You did not die, but you could have. Nyvasu Mweri is a dangerous place. The Burong lives there. And the people of the Burong live there. We told you that before you went. Yet you went there so that we could be safe. And you did all this because God loves us and you love us? That is a good thing. I say, that is a very good thing."

The old chief stood to his feet. "I will think about what you have said. I will think about your Jesus. And I will come to your meetings. I think my people need this Jesus. I think I do too." He walked away quietly.

Rev. Derrington looked at Dr. Walker, and they both smiled. This expedition was worth the trouble after all!

When the party reached the mission station, Mrs. Johnson immediately set to work on Dr. Walker's wounds. She frowned when she saw the deep slashes. She gave him a strong sedative, then waited for him to become groggy. Then she cleaned the wound, stitched the four deepest cuts, bandaged his leg and gave Dr. Walker an antibiotic injection.

It was late that night before he woke up. He was groggy, but his leg felt better than it had for days. He sat up on the bed. Just then, Rev. Derrington came to the door of the infirmary. "Oh, Sam, you're up! Feeling better?"

"Yes, quite," said Dr. Walker. "My leg feels a lot better, but my arm hurts now."

Rev. Derrington laughed and walked to the scientist's bedside. "Mrs. Johnson loves needles," he joked. "She gave you a shot—some kind of antibiotic."

Dr. Walker nodded. "I hate needles, but after

what I've been through this week, I won't complain."

"So what now?"

"What do you mean?"

"Well, simply that you've pretty much finished what you came here to do. The villagers have accepted us as belonging to them. That's something that might never have happened if you hadn't come. So you've accomplished what you came for. At least, you've finished the task I had in mind when I asked you to come. I'm extremely grateful to you for that. But you don't seem satisfied. So what's next?"

"Well, I have to catch my train at Chemechi in five days, but somehow I think that's not what you're getting at. Tell me what's on your mind."

"I want to know if you're coming back."

Dr. Walker was quiet for several minutes. "I'd like to find out—" he said simply.

"Find out whether the Burong, or monster, or Leviathan..."

Dr. Walker nodded. "I want to know if it's really there."

Rev. Derrington pulled up a chair and sat down. "I thought you would feel that way. You're too good a scientist to let a question like that go unanswered. Mr. Johnson told me about your pictures, about the things you found and about the answers you didn't find. I know you probably

154

want to put together an expedition with the proper equipment to find definitive answers about the Leviathan—or at least about these people and their dragon cult. But I'd like to ask you not to. At least wait awhile."

"Why?" asked Dr. Walker, moving to the edge of his cot. "Why shouldn't I come back and prove or disprove the existence of the Burong?"

Rev. Derrington folded his hands across one knee. "What would happen to the mission work if you brought in a full-fledged expedition?"

Dr. Walker looked toward the village. He settled back on the cot. "I don't know," he said at last.

"Let me tell you," said Rev. Derrington. "The people of the village have developed a trust in me. They know now that the Johnsons and I came here to help them. They believe you did too. Now, suppose you were to bring in a team of researchers, photographers, anthropologists, zoologists and the like. Don't you think that trust would be eroded? I think it would evaporate altogether.

"And what about our green friends at Nyvasu? They need the Gospel too. If you bring an expedition in here, we will never see them again. They'll just fade back into the jungle, and we'll lose our opportunity to reach them for Christ."

"But, Clyde, isn't it also important to know whether there really is a creature here that might be the biblical Leviathan?" asked Dr. Walker. "Just think how strong that evidence would be that the Bible is true. Don't you think that counts for something?"

"Not really," answered the missionary. "The Bible doesn't need proving. It doesn't need anybody to provide evidence that it is true. It simply is. Whether we choose to believe it or not is not going to change because of a thing like this. People believe the Bible by faith, or they do not accept it at all—evidence or no evidence. You should know that by now. And even if it were important to find the Leviathan, such a thing pales when compared to the importance of reaching these people for Christ. I know you're a good scientist, Sam, but I also know you're a good Christian. Surely you can see that I'm right. Solving one of the world's last mysteries is not as important as reaching one of the world's last unevangelized peoples."

Just then Mrs. Johnson came into the infirmary and hurried Rev. Derrington out. She insisted that Dr. Walker lie down and sleep.

"You can talk more tomorrow, but for now, you're going to bed." And there was no arguing with her.

Dr. Walker went to sleep that night with Rev. Derrington's words burning in his ears. His instincts were to find out, to prove that the

Leviathan existed—or prove that it didn't. Personally, he believed that it did. And he knew he would not rest until he knew for sure. But he couldn't argue with the missionary's logic. "Solving one of the world's last mysteries is not as important as reaching one of the world's last unevangelized peoples." That was true. So he would wait. If the people at Nyvasu Mweri were someday reached with the Gospel, perhaps he could return. Until then, well, what would he do? What would he tell the people back home?

Chapter 14
DECISIONS

Dr. Walker settled back into the deep cushions of his first-class seat. *This plane ride will be enjoyable,* he thought to himself. After three bruising days of riding in a litter and three days of bus, train and small airplane rides, this ride across the Atlantic would be a piece of cake. When the pilot had discovered that he was injured, he had insisted that he take an empty first-class seat. Dr. Walker determined that he would write the airline a note of thanks.

What a trip it had been! He reviewed the events of the past month for the fortieth time. It seemed hard to believe that it had happened—that such a place even existed. He was actually looking forward to the remaining months of winter back home in Michigan! How could two such diverse places exist on the same planet?

As he reclined his seat, troubled thoughts took over. He still had not answered to his own satisfaction the questions that had been raised in his mind. He knew, of course, that he would not lead an expedition back to Nyvasu anytime in the near future. He had as much as promised Clyde Derrington that he would not. But what about later? And what was he to tell the people at the university—and the people who had put up the money for the trip? He was concerned that if the story of his expedition were told, others would mount an expedition and cause problems for the mission. But he could not lie. What could he say?

He thought of the chief who had come to the mission the morning of his departure.

"I am going with you to Chemechi," he had said. "You have been very helpful to my people. I will let nothing happen to you. I will walk beside your litter all the way." And he had. He had overseen every part of that three-day hike. He had brought food and water. He had carried the equipment pack himself. "You are always my friend," he said. "Because of you, I now belong to Jesus." How thrilling to hear these words from the chief himself!

And then there was Bolgi. He had insisted on being one of the carriers all the way from Marjao to Chemechi. He had carried Dr. Walker fifty-two miles! *I ought to tell our head football coach about that guy,* he thought to himself. *I could probably get him on scholarship!*

Thinking about school led to thoughts of Peter. In September, Peter would be coming to the States to live with Dr. and Mrs. Walker. He would be attending the university. Dr. Walker sincerely hoped that Peter would follow his interest in science. *We need bright kids like that at the university—kids who have good heads on their shoulders, but who also love Christ and want to live for Him,* he thought. *Not nearly enough of those kind around.*

But always his thoughts came back to his decision. *What will I say?* He thought of the evidence he had collected. He had photographs of the lake, the cave, the statues of the serpent and crocodile. He was sure his photographs of the cave paintings and the dragon altar were worth a fortune to some scientific journal. And he had his diary, which he had completed on the train. Even the tabloids would have paid dearly for his story and the pictures!

But that was beside the point. The important thing was, that kind of evidence couldn't be ignored. Something—Leviathan, dragon, dinosaur—had once lived at Nyvasu Mweri. Whether it still did or not was the question, and it was the most important question. Yet if he told anyone—anyone at all—he risked public notoriety. Then if he denied it—well, he couldn't deny it. And if he didn't, somebody would launch an all-out expedition. Look what had happened at Loch Ness. That lake had been scoured from top to bottom— literally. And if that happened at Nyvasu Mweri, the mission work would be hurt, if not destroyed.

What could I say?

These thoughts continued to haunt him all the way to New York. There, after a short delay, he boarded another plane. This one was going to take him home!

As he sat on the plane he asked God to help him with his decision. In just a few short hours he would have to tell his story. The photographs and his journal were real evidence. And they were a danger to the Marjao mission.

He made his decision: *I must destroy the evidence.*

He reached for his carry-on bag and found the small packet containing his film. He dug through the bag until he found his yellow legal pad. He walked back to the galley of the plane and asked the flight attendant for a bottle opener. He went into the rest room, tore the legal pad into small pieces and threw them into the trash can. He used the bottle opener to pry the ends off his 35-mm film canisters, pulled the film from each canister and unrolled it, exposing it to the lights of the rest room; then he threw them into the trash can. This done, he took the bottle opener back to the galley and returned to his seat.

He felt a little light-headed. It had been a difficult thing to do, but now he was glad it was over. It couldn't be undone. Only one thing left to do.

Reaching under his seat, he took out his notebook computer, turned it on and opened the file marked "Journal." He hesitated. Could he really destroy his journal? After all, there wasn't a printout of it. It was only a file on his computer. He could password-protect it, and no one could get at it. Nobody would know about it except him.

It was not an easy decision. He sat there pondering it for an hour. He read the journal and tried to see if there was some way to edit it to tell the story and yet protect the mission work.

His leg was hurting. *Well,* he thought, *if I do dump the journal and decide to tell anybody about the trip, I have some proof—nineteen parallel scars on my leg!* He asked the flight attendant for a glass of water and took some more pain pills. Then he realized he was stalling.

When the "Fasten Seat Belts" sign came on and the captain announced that they would be landing in twenty minutes, Dr. Walker knew the time had come to act. Then the thought came to him, *Solving one of the world's last mysteries is not as important as reaching one of the world's last unevangelized peoples.*

He had to do it now, he knew, or he would never do it. He selected the file and the backup file. Then, just before the wheels of the plane touched the runway, he pressed "Delete." There! It was done!

The hard drive clicked, and then the message came on the screen:

Are you sure? y/n

For a complete list of books available from the Sword of the Lord, write to Sword of the Lord Publishers, P. O. Box 1099, Murfreesboro, Tennessee 37133.

(800) 251-4100
(615) 893-6700
FAX (615) 848-6943
www.swordofthelord.com